MARGIN OF ERROR

FOG LAKE SUSPENSE, BOOK 2

CHRISTY BARRITT

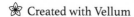

COMPLETE BOOK LIST

Squeaky Clean Mysteries:

#14 Cold Case: Clean Sweep
While You Were Sweeping, A Riley Thomas Spinoff

The Sierra Files:
#1 Pounced
#2 Hunted
#3 Pranced
#4 Rattled
#5 Caged (coming soon)

The Gabby St. Claire Diaries (a Tween Mystery series):
The Curtain Call Caper
The Disappearing Dog Dilemma
The Bungled Bike Burglaries

The Worst Detective Ever
#1 Ready to Fumble
#2 Reign of Error
#3 Safety in Blunders
#4 Join the Flub
#5 Blooper Freak
#6 Flaw Abiding Citizen
#7 Gaffe Out Loud
#8 Joke and Dagger (coming soon)

Raven Remington

Attempt to Locate

First Degree Murder

Dead on Arrival

Plan of Action

Carolina Moon Series

Home Before Dark

Gone By Dark

Wait Until Dark

Light the Dark

Taken By Dark

Suburban Sleuth Mysteries:

Death of the Couch Potato's Wife

Fog Lake Suspense:

Edge of Peril

Margin of Error

Cape Thomas Series:

Dubiosity

Disillusioned

Distorted

Standalone Romantic Mystery:

The Good Girl

Suspense:

Imperfect
The Wrecking

Standalone Romantic-Suspense:
Keeping Guard
The Last Target
Race Against Time
Ricochet
Key Witness
Lifeline
High-Stakes Holiday Reunion
Desperate Measures
Hidden Agenda
Mountain Hideaway
Dark Harbor
Shadow of Suspicion
The Baby Assignment
The Cradle Conspiracy (coming soon)

Nonfiction:
Characters in the Kitchen

Changed: True Stories of Finding God through Christian Music (out of print)

The Novel in Me: The Beginner's Guide to Writing and Publishing a Novel (out of print)

1

Hunger and anger battled inside him like two storm fronts colliding. A violent friction clashed in his very soul.

A low growl formed in his chest. No one else heard it. But he felt it rumble inside him, stirring up emotions best left dormant.

Two men sat perched on a fallen tree. Beer cans surrounded them. Joints dangled from their mouths. Lewd jokes passed between them.

His hands fisted. They had no respect. He was so tired of people not caring. Of people acting like they owned the world.

They didn't.

Men like these didn't deserve this mountain. They didn't understand the land.

Most of all, they didn't belong here in his territory.

The growl inside him grew louder, harder to ignore.

As he blended with the shadows, his fingers dug into the tree in front of him. Each scratch of his skin against the rough wood sent a shiver of delight through him and made him feel more alive.

Do it, an internal voice told him.

Another voice reminded him that this wasn't right. Told him he should leave and let law enforcement take care of these hoodlums.

But he couldn't. He was fully committed right now. He had a mission, a purpose.

He closed his eyes and took a deep breath. The woodsy scent of the trees filled his nostrils. Barren branches clacked against each other above him. The cold wind slapped his face. Each refueled him and confirmed the task before him.

He would do whatever it took to protect this land.

He'd been watching these two for the past hour, and they had no idea.

They thought they were alone out there. Hiking. Camping. Being men.

These *boys* would soon find out that there was nothing manly about them.

Soon, they'd be reduced to the beginnings of

dust. They'd go back to where they came from. Back to the dirt.

And no one would care.

A smile stretched across his face at the thought, and he salivated for the moment he could send his message loud and clear. It had been too long since he'd stood up for what he believed.

Now was the time. He'd lain dormant, but he was like a bear coming out of hibernation.

One man tossed an empty beer can into the brush.

His hands fisted with anger.

The boys had no respect. For people. For this sacred place.

At the thought, his anger burned as red hot as the summer sun.

And suddenly he could wait no longer.

Extending his claws, he flew from his hiding spot like a cougar pouncing on its prey. He was out for blood, and he would get what he wanted. He pitied anyone who tried to stop him.

B rynlee Parker's muscles ached. Her lungs squeezed. Her skin felt numb with cold.

Why had she ever thought this hike was a good idea? She was only an hour in and already felt winded, tired, and miserable.

The man at the camping store had been right. This was no hike for beginners. Her whole life people had told her she couldn't. Now she was telling herself she could.

She paused on the trail long enough to sag against a chilly boulder and catch her breath. A cold breeze swept around her, reminding her that she should have trained more.

I'm doing this for you, Dad.

This hike was his dream, his wish. Brynlee had to see this through in honor of his memory.

That was the only reason she'd come here to Fog Lake, Tennessee. This location was beautiful. More than beautiful. The town was tucked away into the mountains, not far from the tourist hub known as Gatlinburg. Though Brynlee had just begun to explore the area, something magical seemed to tinge the air.

This journey up the mountainside would be a catharsis. It would be healing. A time to find herself.

She'd waited for too long to take the leap.

Maybe, in the process, her dad's family would finally accept her, and Brynlee would have the support system she'd always longed for.

Voices caught her ear. She glanced around, trying to pinpoint where the sound came from. Through the trees below, she spotted two hikers perched on a fallen log. They appeared to have ventured off the trail and set up camp near the creek below.

She narrowed her eyes as recognition filled her.

Those two.

Brynlee had stopped by the trailhead last evening just as they had been setting out. The two college boys had crudely asked her to join them.

She'd refused.

They'd been pushy, and their breath reeked of alcohol. It wouldn't surprise her if their backpacks were mostly full of beer. Their reasons for coming up this mountain weren't the same as Brynlee's. Not by any stretch of the imagination.

Before the men could take it any further, she'd climbed in her SUV and gotten far away.

Brynlee stared down at them now and shook her head. The two sat shooting the breeze. Parts of their conversation drifted up to her, confirming they were jerks. Bona fide jerks.

She'd been around plenty of guys like them in her twenty-eight years.

Based on their spilled backpacks and the strewn trash around them, they'd made themselves a little too comfortable. Some people came here to enjoy nature. Others came for the privacy nature afforded —privacy to do things like getting high. One of her interior design clients had spent time hiking the Appalachian Trail and had told her stories.

Brynlee needed to keep moving. The last thing she wanted was for them to see an opportunity that she didn't desire. She'd dealt with enough situations like that growing up.

While her mom had been singing on grimy stages at rinky-dink bars, Brynlee had been left to fend for herself. And too many drunk men had seen opportunities, especially as Brynlee had grown older.

Brynlee dragged in a few more ragged breaths. She just needed a couple more minutes of rest before she continued hiking. She could do this. She *would* do this.

There was only one way to get to the top of this mountain, and that was on foot.

She let her backpack slide from her shoulders to the ground.

Nothing had prepared her for this hike. For the thin, cold air. The uphill climb. The narrow path riddled with rocks and roots.

And again—this was the easy part.

She pulled out her water bottle and took a long sip.

Five minutes. That's all the time you've got, and then you start again.

Parkers don't give up.

Brynlee's mom had unsuccessfully followed her dreams until the day she died. Brynlee pushed aside the fact that nearly every day of her childhood, she had resented the fact her mom had pursued such hopeless dreams.

Maybe giving up was a good idea sometimes.

She glanced down at the two other hikers again. She sat in a shadowed area, so the two men probably had no idea she was here. As they laughed raucously at another perverse joke, it only confirmed her initial thought. *Jerks.*

Just like most of the men who'd ever been in her life.

She couldn't sit here and listen to them anymore. She needed to keep moving.

Brynlee started to stand. But, as she did, a new sound cut through the air.

A sickening roar.

Her muscles lurched.

Screams echoed over the mountain.

Yells.

Shouts of terror.

Slowly, she pivoted toward the men.

Her eyes widened in horror when she saw a beast emerge from the woods. His claws sliced into one man's neck. Blood spurted. The man fell to the ground.

The other man stumbled back, trying to get away. But the beast lunged toward him, capturing him.

Brynlee's eyes remained locked on the nightmare in front of her.

The beast—that was all she knew to call whatever that thing was—demolished the other man, leaving him like a limp, bleeding ragdoll on the forest floor.

She swallowed a scream.

What in the world was happening . . . ?

Leave, Brynlee. Leave. Before it sees you.

An internal nudging finally took root in her head.

Why was she just sitting here? She needed to go. Now.

As a surge of adrenaline rushed through her, she jumped to her feet.

Her shoe hit a pebble.

She held her breath as the stone tumbled down the mountainside.

Toward the scene below.

The beast looked up at her, its eyes savage and hungry.

Fear exploded inside her.

Brynlee took off in a run, knowing if the beast caught her, she'd face a certain—and painful —death.

"And then Danny Axon threw up all over her. I mean, *all* over her. His date was horrified—as was everyone else in Hanky's. Who am I kidding? Everyone else was laughing hysterically. The man deserves a good dose of humility!"

Boone Wilder listened as Chigger Wati continued on, his chubby face animated with every new detail. It wasn't that Boone didn't care about his employee's story. His mind was just in a different place right now.

March 26 was always a difficult day. At least, it

had been for the past five years. Add to that the fact that the future of Falling Timbers Camping and General Store was on the rocks, and he was in a rotten mood. He had employees who depended on him. What would he do if this place was shut down?

Boone uncrossed his arms and grabbed a dart. Aiming carefully, he drew his arm back and launched.

It hit the bullseye.

"So, how about that woman who came in here earlier?" Chigger said, undeterred by Boone's lack of response just moments earlier. The man's nickname wasn't an accident. No, Chigger had a tendency to get under people's skin and irritate them to no end. But his deep, infectious laugh made up for his otherwise grating lack of social awareness.

"Which woman?" Boone asked, throwing another dart.

"The one who asked if we had any organic snacks for the trail or if we had any tips for hiking to Dead Man's Bluff."

Boone remembered the customer well. In fact, he'd been thinking about her since she left. It was hard to forget the woman—and not just because she was beautiful. She also seemed stubborn and hardheaded.

"You mean Ms. LL Bean?" Boone asked.

Chigger laughed. "She's the one. Not your typical hiker."

"Not at all." The woman had looked like she'd gone on a shopping spree at an expensive clothing outfitter just so she could look good in her puffy vest, jeans, and expensive boots as she posed for social media photos. "Hope she's doing okay out there."

Boone had tried to tell the woman that going alone was a bad idea. She had the wrong gear. Horrible hiking boots. No clue how to get help if she hurt herself while alone on the trail. There was hardly any cell phone reception up that way.

He threw another dart, a little harder than he should have.

That woman wouldn't make it three miles.

"I don't know what some people are thinking." Chigger leaned with his elbows on the wooden counter near the register. "But it's a free world, so people can make their own choices—stupid or not."

That might be true, but Boone couldn't help but think he should have tried harder to stop the woman. Or told her he could act as a guide on her trip. But she'd been determined to go today, and Boone couldn't just drop everything he was doing and leave. She should have planned better.

So why did he feel guilty?

As the bell above the door jangled, Boone turned toward the sound. A rush of cold mountain air bellowed into the room as the door opened. Someone collapsed in the entry.

Boone sucked in a breath.

Ms. LL Bean. She was back.

And something was terribly wrong.

The woman's eyes looked wild, almost crazy. Her blonde hair sprang out from beneath her hat. Her clothes were torn. She could hardly catch her breath as she bent forward in front of them, terror stretched across her face.

"Please . . . help me."

Boone rushed around the counter and caught her before she completely crumpled. He had no idea what had happened, but he recognized the shock on her features. It was like he'd feared—something bad had happened to her on that trail.

"Chigger, call 911," he barked. "Now."

Boone waited until his employee grabbed the phone before he turned his attention back to the woman. She appeared shaken and scratched, but he didn't see any life-threatening injuries.

But emotionally . . . that was an entirely different story. What had happened to this woman to shake her up like this?

"Come on back to my office," he coaxed. "Sit down. I'll get you some water."

She didn't argue. Maybe she couldn't. Her limbs shook so badly.

As Boone helped her stand upright, her gaze swerved behind her. She clung to him, terror seeming to pulse through her as she quickly gasped air.

She was expecting someone else to barge in behind her, wasn't she? Someone dangerous.

Boone exchanged a look with Chigger and then nodded toward the store's entrance.

As soon as Chigger got off the phone, his employee would need to guard the door. At least until Boone knew what was going on. What had happened to scare this woman like this? Had someone attacked her?

"What's your name?" Boone asked.

"Brynlee." Her teeth chattered, and Boone feared she was succumbing to shock.

"Brynlee, I'm Boone. We didn't officially introduce ourselves to each other earlier."

Boone led the woman to the crammed office in the corner of the rustic building that housed his business. He sat her in a chair across from his desk and knelt in front of her.

"Take a few deep breaths," Boone said, relying on his survival training. He worked as a volunteer here on the trail and had an EMT certification, not to mention his military background.

Brynlee raked some stray hairs away from her face,

breathed in and then out. Her breaths were shaky, along with the rest of her body. After a few minutes of controlled breathing, she seemed a little calmer.

"Can you tell me what happened?" Boone locked gazes with her, trying to keep her focused.

She swallowed hard and barely managed a nod.

"I was . . . I was hiking. I took a break and saw these men down below sitting on a log, and then this animal beast thing came out of nowhere and attacked the men. It was so horrible." Her voice cracked as her rush of words ended with a quick intake of air.

Boone waited for her to continue, waited for her to make sense.

"I tried to run, but it saw me." She rubbed her throat as her voice continued to crack. "If it caught me . . . I knew it would kill me too."

She buried her face in her hands as a new round of sobs overtook her.

What in the world was this woman talking about? What she said sounded like nonsense.

Animal beast thing?

"So, you saw some kind of attack?" he clarified.

A half sob escaped, but she seemed to swallow the rest. "It was horrible."

"Were you . . . on the trail to Dead Man's Bluff?"

"Yes." Her voice cracked.

All that place amounted to was a whole lot of heartache and trouble.

Boone knew firsthand.

Dread pooled in his stomach as he waited to hear the rest of her story. He knew one thing: trouble was brewing on that mountain again. And trouble on Dead Man's Bluff always had fatal results.

3

Brynlee tried to focus on her breathing and remain calm as she prepared to tell her story again. The sheriff sat in front of her—Sheriff Wilder. The man couldn't be that much older than she was, and he had dark hair and perceptive eyes. Apparently, Boone was his brother.

Speaking of Boone . . .the man had been infuriating when she'd come into the store earlier. She was so tired of men seeing her as a target, as easy prey, or an easy punchline.

She was so much more than that.

Don't find yourself whole in the glance of a man. Find yourself whole by your own hand.

The lyrics to one of her mother's songs floated into her mind. Funny, her mom hadn't taken her own advice. She'd switched from one man to another like some people changed clothes.

And she'd been miserable.

Brynlee's trembles had calmed some, but she still felt everything spinning around her. She took a sip from the water bottle Boone had given her.

"Tell me what happened," Sheriff Wilder coaxed, pen poised over the notepad in his hands. "Start from the beginning."

Brynlee took another sip of water before repeating her story.

Nausea pooled in her stomach as she replayed the moments in her mind. It had been so violent. So horrible. Something she would never forget, no matter how much counseling she might go through.

"Did he have a knife?" Sheriff Wilder asked. "A gun?"

She shook her head, the trembles growing deeper again.

"No, he used . . ." She swallowed hard. "He used his claws."

"His claws?" The sheriff leaned back and narrowed his eyes.

Images of the beast flooded her mind. Each picture of him made her flinch as if she'd physically been slapped.

"Yeah, he was this . . . I don't know how to describe him." Brynlee swung her head back and forth, knowing she was going to sound crazy. "He was like a beast. Hairy and big. Fast. Vicious."

The sheriff tilted his head. "What do you mean? Was it a man or an animal?"

She shuddered again, asking herself that same question. Every time she replayed it . . . she wasn't sure.

"He had fur all over his body. At first, I thought it was a bear. But then it rose up on two legs and started attacking the men." Her voice cracked.

"How do you know it wasn't a bear?" Boone straightened from where he'd been leaning in the doorway, but his voice sounded surprisingly inquisitive instead of aggravating. "They can stand on their hind legs."

"It didn't stand like a bear," she said. "I don't know. I realize I don't make sense. I'm not an expert on these things."

Brynlee squeezed her eyes shut, trying desperately to get a grip. She was accomplished. Had two degrees. Was by all worldly standards successful. Today's tragedy made her feel like a bumbling fool. Like everything had been turned upside down.

She drew in a shaky breath before continuing. "It was just . . . I don't know. I realized I had to move. When I stood, a small rock tumbled down the hill. This . . . this beast . . . looked up at me. I thought I saw a human face, covered in some kind of paint, but human. I still can't make sense of it myself."

The sheriff nodded slowly. "Okay, we'll get back to that again later. What happened next?"

"I did the only thing I could think of. I took off running. I knew he was going to come after me."

"And did he?" Sheriff Wilder asked.

"He did. But I had a head start. I ran back the way I came from, knowing I'd be better off going down the mountain instead of up. I'd only hiked for about an hour, so I knew I wasn't too far away."

"Did you lose him?" the sheriff asked.

"No, he was behind me. But he wasn't as fast as I thought he would be. I think I had enough of a head start that I was able to escape. I reached my car, but I realized . . . I didn't have my keys. I left them in my bag on the mountainside." She flinched at the thought.

There were things inside that bag. Things she couldn't lose—like her father's ashes. And there were other things, things she didn't want anyone else to see.

"I had no choice but to keep running," she continued. "I looked back into the woods, and I saw him. He stood there, behind some brush, just staring at me."

A cry escaped her again, and the sheriff handed her a tissue. "It's okay. Take your time."

Brynlee wiped her eyes, nodded, and gulped in another breath. "This was the first place I came to. Honestly, I can't believe I'm still alive. I just knew I was going to die. That he was going to catch me and kill me like he killed those other men."

"Why were you headed to Dead Man's Bluff?" the sheriff asked.

She shrugged. "I promised my father that I'd spread his ashes there. He passed away four months ago."

"I'm sorry for your loss," Sheriff Wilder said. "We're going to need to send a team to the area where you saw this crime happen. Can you tell us where you were on the trail? It's thirteen miles to get to Dead Man's Bluff and back."

"I . . . I don't know." She shrugged. "Like I said, I'd been hiking for maybe an hour. I might be able to show you."

"That's a terrible idea," Boone said.

"I have to agree with my brother," the sheriff said. "You're not in great shape right now. Time is of the essence also. We don't want wildlife to destroy the scene."

"I can do it." Some strength returned to Brynlee's voice. "I can."

Boone spoke in a low tone as he said, "Brynlee, you don't know what's out there or what you might be facing."

"I need to go." Her voice came out soft but firm. "I'll be safe with you all."

Sheriff Wilder exchanged a look with Boone, who nodded at him.

Brynlee knew the truth. She couldn't tell them how to find the bodies. She was going to have to show them. Plus, she needed her backpack. Needed to get it before other people started rummaging through the contents and her secret escaped.

Yes, her reasons for coming here had been twofold.

"Let me call my team in then, and we'll get going," the sheriff said. "In the meantime, can I speak with you, Boone? Outside?"

Boone's throat felt tight as he stepped onto the porch-like entrance to his store with his brother. A fresh, piney scent swept across the rocky ground with the wind, sending a scattering of dried leaves against the roughhewn log siding of his store. Though the sun looked cheery and bright, cool air invigorated everything around them.

Chigger remained inside, and Brynlee sat in Boone's office still.

Boone knew a little more now. The woman's

name was Brynlee Parker. She was twenty-eight years old. From Pennsylvania. Single.

Dead Man's Bluff seemed like an odd choice to spread ashes, considering how unforgiving the area was.

There was a reason the overlook had been given the name. Deaths had occurred in the area. Too many deaths. Most from hiking or climbing accidents. A few from wild animal attacks. One from someone who'd gotten lost in the area for too many days.

Boone knew where this conversation with his brother would most likely go.

"Do you think she realized before heading up to Dead Man's Bluff that it's one of the most treacherous hikes on the East Coast?" Luke asked.

"Great question." Boone had tried to warn her, but she hadn't listened. Not that this was a time to say, "I told you so." But some people were just too strong-willed for their own good.

"What do you make of this animal beast thing she mentioned?" Luke stared at Boone, studying his reaction. It was no secret that Boone knew these mountains better than most. That he spent most of his free time hiking the trails and fishing and camping.

His dad had taught him to hunt, how to track animals, how to survive out there. He'd taught Luke also, but Luke had never been as interested as Boone.

"I mean, there's been a rumor in the mountains for years that some kind of beast existed. No one thinks it's true. She probably saw a bear. It makes the most sense, especially when she described how those men died."

Luke shifted and turned away from the glaring sun. "Boone, I'd like for you to go with us to the location."

Boone stepped back and shook his head. "I don't know about that."

"I know you hate that area. I do. But I could really use your help."

"What can I do that would help?"

"Keep an eye on Brynlee, for starters. She doesn't seem like she's in any shape to make this hike. And you know the area better than anyone else. We could use your expertise."

Boone let out a long, slow breath, trying to think of a reason not to go. "Who's going to run the store?"

"Chigger can do it. Besides, hardly anyone is out at this time of year. You and I both know business is slow here in Fog Lake in March."

Boone searched desperately for another excuse. But he came up with nothing. "Fine. I'll go. But only for you."

"Thanks. How long will it take you to get geared up?"

"I can be ready in thirty."

"Perfect. Let's meet then."

Boone had stepped away when Luke called his name again. He paused and turned toward his brother.

"I know today is a hard day for you," Luke said. "None of us have forgotten Kat, though. I wish she was here to celebrate turning twenty-seven."

Boone swallowed hard, his throat suddenly burning. "Thank you."

A new sense of dread captured him. Boone hadn't been up to the summit of Dead Man's Bluff since the incident with Katherine . . . and he dreaded the gut-wrenching memories he'd face on the very day he was supposed to be celebrating her birth.

4

Brynlee stood on the side of the road near where the emergency vehicles had parked. Sunlight streamed through the high treetops around her, and the mountains seemed to surround her like a fortress—or a prison.

Right now, she waited for the rest of the crew to arrive and for the sheriff to dole out his instructions. She leaned against the truck she'd ridden over in, trying to contend with her thoughts.

Every time Brynlee closed her eyes, images of the horrible event she'd witnessed filled her mind.

That . . . that . . . thing coming out from the middle of nowhere. Attacking those hikers. Leaving their dead bodies there.

And then chasing her.

She'd been sure she would be captured and her

body torn apart. That her remains would be ravaged and found days later.

A tremble started in her core again and spread to her extremities.

This all seemed like a nightmare she would wake up from.

But there was no waking up.

Those men really had died. And now she was going to return to the place where it had happened.

Brynlee had told the sheriff that she could lead them there, and she hoped her words were true. But her thoughts felt so scattered. Fear had dug its talons into her very being, and those talons were sinking deeper by the moment.

"You ready for this?"

She glanced up at Boone. The man had been so irritating when she'd met him at the store this morning. He seemed to think he knew what was best for her as he insisted she shouldn't do the hike alone.

His cocky attitude had caused a surge of frustration to rush through her. She hated it when people underestimated her or judged her without knowing anything about her.

Most of all, she was tired of listening to people who were determined to tear her down instead of build her up.

That fact put her on edge right now. Sure, the man had been kind when she'd rushed inside after she witnessed the attack. But that didn't mean he was noble.

Brynlee wasn't sure where he'd come from just now, but she nodded at his question. *You ready for this?* In truth, she wasn't ready for anything. But what other choice did she have?

Boone thrust something at her. "Here's a backpack you can use. It has some water and snacks in it. Organic."

"Thank you."

"Are you staying somewhere local?"

She blinked again, wishing she could clear her head. She had a feeling that was exactly what Boone was trying to do—distract her from her otherwise burdensome thoughts.

"I'm . . . I rented a place not too far away. A chalet."

She'd arrived just yesterday with barely enough time to check in, buy some groceries, and take care of a little business. She'd cleared her schedule and told her clients that she'd return in a week.

She'd felt surprisingly excited to be here.

How quickly things had changed.

Boone stepped closer and dipped his head. "It's going to be okay."

His voice somehow sounded convincing, and a wave of comfort washed over her. Maybe he was right. Maybe everything would be okay, even though it didn't feel like it right now.

She hoped her gaze showed her gratitude because her voice seemed to dry up.

"Okay, everyone." Sheriff Wilder rounded up the crew. "Let's head out. The sooner we find the location of these bodies, the better."

From what Brynlee could tell, the trek would include herself, the sheriff, one deputy, Boone, two park rangers, a game warden, and a state police officer. Everyone had donned hiking boots and backpacks and weapons. There were lots of weapons. Handguns. Rifles. She'd even heard someone mention a dart gun.

"What about the Skookum?" the deputy asked. His name tag read "Cruise," and he was on the younger side. Even his actions seemed to indicate he was a rookie. He continually looked to the sheriff for guidance, repeatedly wiped his hands on his pants, and nervously glanced around as if fearful.

Sheriff Wilder scowled. "He's a legend. Not real. I think we all know that."

"But—"

"No more questions about the Skookum. We need to get moving. I'll lead. Boone, you bring up the rear. Got it?"

Everyone nodded in affirmation.

They started toward the trailhead in the

distance. The path was marked with a brown sign that told the hike's distance, the elevation, and the level of difficulty. However, the path to Dead Man's Bluff only started where it branched off from this official trail and onto an unofficial one.

Her throat went dry as she stared at the small opening through the forest. Ordinarily, it would be breathtaking with the little stream that trickled beside it. Almost from the start, this trail sloped upward, an incline that required much more physical aptness than she'd anticipated.

Brynlee's legs ached as she looked at it, reminding her of what would be required to do this. It was a near miracle she'd gotten as far as she had the first time. That she'd managed to escape down this trail without falling and breaking her neck.

Boone walked a steady pace behind her. His hands gripped the straps of his backpack, and he looked like he'd done this a million times before. In fact, he looked like he belonged out here—in a good, comfortable way.

Then again, he also acted like he owned the world.

He was handsome enough to have that complex. His messy honey-blond hair, his scruffy I-don't-care beard, his startling green eyes. Even in this stressful situation, something about him screamed fun-loving and easy-going.

"Thanks for everything you've done." She glanced back at him then tugged at the bill of her trendy trucker-style baseball cap and stared at the steep trail that stretched up into the mountains. "What's the Skookum?"

He shrugged. "It's an old Native American legend. Nothing that I would give much credence too."

"Does this old legend involve someone who looks half-man, half-beast?" She watched Boone's face, watched as his lips pulled down at the sides in a slight frown.

"It's just a legend."

"But I saw it, Boone," she whispered.

Brynlee hadn't imagined what she'd seen, and she didn't care what anyone thought. A creature straight out of her nightmares had invaded reality. Had destroyed two lives. And he'd done so without a moment of hesitation.

"We'll get it figured out," he said. "Let's just concentrate on finding the crime scene right now, okay?"

"What if he comes out while we're hiking?" Her lungs tightened at her words, at the thought of seeing the monster again. She couldn't stand the thought of it.

Maybe going up the mountain again wasn't a good idea. Maybe it was a terrible idea.

Brynlee stopped there on the trail, trying to collect herself before a panic attack hit her. But her lungs felt like they were seizing up, and, as hard as she tried, she couldn't seem to force air into them.

Boone stopped beside her and placed a hand on her arm. His touch jolted her back to reality, jolted her body back into function.

He leaned toward her, his voice surprisingly gentle as he said, "You don't have to do this."

She pulled in a deep breath, grateful her lungs worked properly again. "Yes, I do."

"Why? Why do you have to do this?" He tugged at the knit cap he wore, pulling it over his ears. A few stray waves escaped from the edges, making him look like the poster child for the all-American boy next door—only all grown up.

Brynlee couldn't tell him the real reason. She would become an outcast here in Fog Lake if she did. Her dad had told her all about what happened last time he'd come into town. Brynlee would learn from his mistakes.

"To prove to myself that I can do it," she finally said, trying to keep the fear from her voice.

"Have it your way then."

She continued hiking up the trail. This was the easy part. Apparently, after the two miles, the trail split. One path was treacherous and required climbing equipment. The other path was longer but not quite as steep and difficult.

That was the path she'd been planning to take. She hadn't made it that far, however.

She should have never tried to do this alone, but not for the reasons she'd originally thought.

A rustling in the woods stopped them in their steps.

Brynlee froze as something burst from the foliage. She prepared herself for a face-to-face encounter with the Skookum, wondering if anyone would mourn her if she died.

Boone heard the rustling leaves. Felt the change in the air. Remembered Brynlee's story.

He pushed Brynlee behind him and braced himself for a fight.

A creature rushed from the brush.

A deer.

The doe darted across the path before disappearing into the woods again.

Everyone's shoulders seemed to relax collectively. They were all on edge right now.

"Let's keep going," Luke said. "No need to get jumpy about Bambi."

Boone glanced back at Brynlee and saw that her

trembles had returned. He had no idea why the woman had insisted on coming.

Nor did he think she was telling the truth. No, she was hiding something about her reasons for being here.

And that made him leery of the woman.

Just what else was she up to, besides spreading her father's ashes? Why else would her gaze be shifty?

Boone had met a lot of people who hiked up here. He'd met a lot of people who attempted these hikes. The people who made him the most nervous were the ones like Brynlee, who optimistically thought they could conquer this trail with little preparation and that they could do so alone. Father's ashes or not, this had been a bad idea.

Boone kept his eyes on the woods as they continued the hike. For a moment, he imagined Brynlee running down the trail, trying to escape from some kind of madman. She must have been terrified.

He knew about that. Knew about life-threatening situations up here. Knew about being desperate to help yet feeling isolated.

Memories pummeled him, but he quickly pushed them away. He couldn't go there mentally. Not now.

"It should be right up here." Brynlee pointed to an area ahead.

Boone glanced at his watch. They'd been walking for about an hour. This should be about right.

"I stopped by some rocks to rest," Brynlee continued. "I set my backpack down there."

He scanned the area ahead. The group in front of them made it difficult to see anything. But Boone knew this landscape well. Knew the boulders and the crags and the cliffs. Even after five years, everything still seemed so fresh.

As the rest of the group paused and pointed at an area down below, he heard Brynlee's quick intake of air beside him.

He jerked his head toward her and saw her staring at the ground, a frown on her face.

Her gaze finally met his. "This is where I stopped for a break. But my backpack . . . it's gone. Do you think the killer took it?"

Boone swallowed hard. The killer? He had no idea.

But the situation Brynlee had found herself in seemed to be growing more dire with every new revelation.

5

Boone remained near the boulders with Brynlee while the rest of the team made their way to the clearing below. He'd only glanced down at the area, but he'd seen enough.

Two dead bodies and a bloody crime scene slashed into the otherwise peaceful landscape. The scene was straight out of a horror movie.

He didn't envy his brother's job right now. Investigating this scene, tracking down the loved ones of these men to inform them of what had happened, trying to get the bodies out of this area . . . it was going to be a long, hard day.

Heaviness settled on him at the thought. When he let himself, he still struggled with how brutal life could be. He struggled with why some people seemed to skate through life relatively unscathed while others had more than their fair share of heartache.

This scene reminded him of all those questions.

Around him, nature seemed to still, sensing something bad had happened. The birds no longer chirped. Even the wind had stopped rustling the tree branches. The crew below spoke in somber tones as they observed the scene and documented each little detail of the area.

Boone turned his gaze from the scene and looked at Brynlee. She stared down below also, tears in her eyes.

This was a lot for anyone to handle, even seasoned law enforcement officers. He was nearly certain this city girl was entirely out of her comfort zone. She had been a trooper when she'd hiked back up here, however. He had to give her credit for that.

He moved, purposefully standing in front of her and blocking her view of what was going on in the distance. He needed to distract her from the horror below. People didn't forget things like this . . . no, these images stayed with people. Changed them—in the very least, in subtle ways.

"You hike a lot?" he asked.

Brynlee frowned and glanced to the side, as if reprimanding herself. "No, not really."

"You planning on being in town long?"

She shrugged. "Just a week."

Boone couldn't stop thinking about what had happened to these men. Whatever it had been, it was violent. Wild animal? A man?

It didn't matter. It was horrific.

And whoever/whatever had done this was still out there.

As soon as the thought entered Boone's mind, the hairs on his neck stood.

He froze and turned.

His gaze scanned the forest around them, looking for any signs of danger.

Trees stared back. Deep shadows. Craggy rock formations.

"What is it?" Brynlee stepped closer, fear seizing her features.

He tried to shrug it off. "Nothing."

There was no need to alarm Brynlee for no reason. She was already traumatized.

"You feel something too, don't you?" Her wide eyes implored him.

Boone's breath caught. He wanted to deny it, but he didn't want to lie. Brynlee deserved better than that. Instead, he remained silent.

His gaze scanned the area again. That feeling remained—the unseen eyes watching them. He couldn't pinpoint where the feeling originated. There were too many shadows. Too many places to hide out here.

Boone didn't know what was going on here, but whatever it was, he didn't like it.

An hour later, Sheriff Wilder asked Boone to take Brynlee back down the trail. He and the recovery crew would be here for a while, and she was no longer needed. The sheriff had asked her to stick around town so he could get an official statement later.

That wouldn't be a problem since she no longer had her car keys.

Boone wasn't very talkative on the way down, but Brynlee saw his gaze constantly scanning everything around them.

He'd seen and felt something also. She didn't care if he admitted it or not. It was the truth.

Whatever had killed those men was still out there. It could be stalking them right now, just waiting for the right minute to pounce.

Her skin crawled at the thought of it. Instinctively, she stepped closer to Boone. Wanted to grasp his arm, to hold on like a lifeline.

But it was better if she kept her distance and maintained her independence.

They finally reached the start of the trail. She looked over at the black SUV that she'd parked on the side of the road there. How she wished she had her keys right now. Her phone.

But someone had taken them.

Most likely, that Skookum.

Boone followed her gaze. "I guess you can't drive yourself back to wherever you're staying."

Brynlee shook her head, realizing that her quest for independence was more like a joke in times like these. "No, I can't."

"I'll give you a ride."

"Thank you." Her voice came out as more of a croak.

Their feet crunched the gravel at the side of the road as they headed toward his truck.

But Brynlee froze as she passed her SUV. She couldn't even find the words. She only gasped and pointed.

Boone looked back and followed her gaze. "What the . . . ?"

He stepped closer and bent toward the vehicle.

But Brynlee didn't need any explanation. She knew what had happened.

The Skookum had found her SUV. And now, a single set of claw marks had been scratched down the length of it on the driver's side.

A clear message had been sent: the beast behind those killings knew who she was.

6

B oone glanced up as the door to the café opened and Brynlee Parker stepped inside.

It had been three hours since he dropped her off at a vacation rental, which was within walking distance of town. A keypad had allowed her to get inside.

As Luke had directed, Boone had documented the scratches on Brynlee's SUV. Since Luke had been busy at the murder site, he said he'd check the vehicle out later.

Boone knew his brother would be at the crime scene well into the night. The victims would need to be carried down the mountainside in body bags, and an autopsy would be done on them. The scene had to be documented, and someone would be sent to track whatever was behind this.

Answers were still a long way from being found.

In the meantime, Boone had come to his favorite restaurant, The Hometown Diner, to grab dinner and try to unwind. Some of his old high school buddies had clustered at a table near the back to talk about basketball and the upcoming whitewater rafting season.

His heart sank when he saw Brynlee step inside, and he lowered the tortilla chip in his hands. It seemed as if there was no avoiding the woman since she'd blown into town.

She scanned the restaurant and blanched when she saw him. She nodded briefly then took a seat by herself on the other side of the dining area.

Boone tried to ignore the fact that she was here and mind his own business as he chatted with his buddies. But his conscience wouldn't let him. Brynlee had just been through something traumatic, and now she sat alone looking like a lost little girl in a strange new world. No one should have to carry that kind of burden alone.

Drawing in a deep breath, he picked up his basket of nachos and his drink before looking at his friends. "Excuse me a minute, guys."

A couple of them wagged their eyebrows but said nothing.

Boone sauntered across the restaurant and slid in across from Brynlee. He would do his civic duty and try to look after a stranger in a strange place. Plus, there was something about the woman that called out to his protective side.

"Do you mind?" Boone asked as Brynlee looked across the table at him.

"I guess it's a little late if I do." The words weren't edged with bitterness but a sense of teasing. She looked like she attempted to smile but didn't quite succeed.

"I can leave." He wouldn't impose if she wanted time alone.

She shrugged. "No, stay. I'm sorry. I'm in a mood."

It had been a long time since Boone had eaten alone with a woman. The town's rumor mill would start soon, the launching point being his friends across the room who stared at them now with sparkling eyes. As "Private Eyes" played on the jukebox, he wished the song didn't ring so true. It did feel like all eyes were on them.

He observed Brynlee from across the table. She'd obviously cleaned up. Her blonde hair now looked clean and glossy as it swished around her shoulders. Her makeup made her face look fresh and bright. Her pink sweater and snug jeans showed off her trim figure.

She looked . . . nice. The realization was an observation and nothing more.

Boone shoved his nachos across the booth toward her. "Would you like some?"

"Thanks, but I'm a vegetarian."

"Good luck finding many things you can eat here in town. Not too many fancy restaurants here."

"I'm used to it. I'll survive."

Her words hung in the air.

Survive.

That's exactly what she had done today in the middle of a harrowing situation. Boone had to admire her for that.

The waitress came, and Brynlee ordered a salad along with a cup of black coffee. Something about her seemed cultured yet surprisingly gentle.

Boone couldn't figure this woman out. Was she a rich brat? A well-dressed woman on a quest to find herself? He didn't know.

As she put away her menu, Boone took another sip of his soda. "I have to admit, I thought you'd probably get out of town as soon as you could. My brother's not making you stay, is he?"

"The sheriff?" She shook her head. "No. I mean, I do have to head into the station tomorrow morning so I can give my official statement."

"And then you'll leave?"

"I don't know."

"I see."

Brynlee shrugged. "What can I say? I've always

been accused of being determined and stubborn. I suppose this trip will prove no different."

"Courage isn't the absence of fear but the ability to face it. Isn't that what they say?"

She almost smiled again. "Yes, I think it's something like that."

Boone shifted, more curious about this woman than ever. "What are you doing here, if you don't mind me asking? Is it just to spread your dad's ashes? Why Dead Man's Bluff, of all places?"

"Yes, it's to spread my dad's ashes. He was very specific before he died. His ashes were to be split four ways, and each of the siblings were to get one-fourth. He wanted part of his remains to be spread at sea, another part kept in the house, the third to be interred at the cemetery, then mine . . . to be carried away by the wind on top of Dead Man's Bluff."

"Sounds like he had a lot of opinions."

Brynlee smiled. "He did. But he also told me before he died that he wanted me to see this mountain. Dad loved it here and spent quite a bit of time in the area when he was younger."

Boone picked up a chip loaded with steak and gooey cheese. "What exactly happened to your dad, if you don't mind me asking?"

"He died of congenital heart failure four months ago." Her voice caught.

"I'm sorry to hear that." All the glibness disappeared from Boone's voice.

She swirled her water, that sad look returning to her eyes. "I've been planning this trip for a while now. I don't want to go back without finishing what I came here to do."

Concern squeezed his gut. "Certainly, you're not thinking about going into those woods again, are you?"

She shrugged. "I don't know yet. I haven't figured it out."

"That hike . . . it isn't for an inexperienced climber." Boone didn't want to tell her what to do, but he'd seen too many people get hurt. He would have figured she got that message loud and clear earlier, but apparently not.

Brynlee bristled, a clear defensiveness washing over her features. "I know."

So many warning bells sounded in his head. This woman . . . Boone wasn't going to be able to convince her to change her mind, was he? Nor was it his place. He hardly knew Brynlee.

But he had a bad feeling in his gut.

"Listen, it's really a bad idea . . ." he said, though he knew his words wouldn't be welcome.

Brynlee leaned closer. "Boone, you've been kind to me, and I appreciate it. But I know your type. You don't have to worry about me."

He raised his brow, curious now. "My type? And what is that?"

She narrowed her eyes. "You really want to know?"

"I really do."

"Fine." She held up a hand and began checking off statements on her fingers. "First, you think you know what's best for everyone around you. You're also a member of the good old boys' club. Everyone here likes you, and you use that to your advantage. You're laid-back, but you know you have influence."

He only grunted and leaned back. "Interesting."

"You like for people to listen to you, to respect your opinion, and you're used to that very thing happening. Especially with women. You know women think you're attractive and they like a strong man who will tell them what to do. I'm not that woman."

He nodded, not arguing with her assessment. But he could play this game also. "I guess I could say that I know your type also."

"And what type is that?" Brynlee's gaze held challenge, and she clearly didn't think he knew what he was talking about.

"Let's see. Your hair has highlights that probably cost more than I make in a month. You wear expensive clothes because you think how a person dresses can make or break the occasion. You think that as long as you have money, you can do whatever you want, including trying to hike up one of the most treacherous trails on the East Coast by yourself and with little preparation."

Her face reddened. Boone had struck a nerve, hadn't he?

He knew he shouldn't push this conversation anymore. He also knew he wasn't welcome here. Brynlee had made that clear.

He stood and offered a nod of apology. "I'll let you eat in peace. I hope you enjoy your stay here. Be safe."

Back at her cabin, Brynlee had changed into her favorite yoga pants, started the gas fireplace in the living room, and made herself a warm cup of tea to help ward the cold away. She only wished Sissy was here—Sissy being her tabby cat. A woman from church was watching her while Brynlee was gone.

As she pulled her legs beneath her on the leather sofa, her conversation with Boone at the diner floated into her mind. The man was certainly interesting. Frustrating. At one moment, he seemed sensitive and compassionate. The next moment arrogant and infuriating.

He didn't know her—no matter what he thought.

Brynlee had noticed he was handsome when she'd first seen him, but she hadn't dwelled on it. She had too many other things on her mind.

But tonight, as they'd sat across from each other, she'd noticed his country boy charm. He seemed to like wearing flannel shirts and jeans that fit just right to show off his physique. But it wasn't in the same way the men back home did.

Boone Wilder was totally comfortable with himself, she realized. He was his own man.

And she could appreciate that.

But the last thing she was looking for was romance or even a remote attraction, especially after Will.

Brynlee had been a fool to ever be with Will. She'd thought if she could date someone with his social standing that her father's family might accept her. But that was never going to happen, was it?

In the process, she'd caught the man with her best friend.

The realization didn't even devastate her. In fact, Brynlee should have seen the writing on the wall long ago. Will hadn't even known her birthday. Or that she loved blueberries. Or that she liked watching sappy old romantic movies.

No, Will had never cared about her. He'd only cared about getting in with her newly discovered family.

Brynlee had come here with purpose, and she couldn't let anything distract her from that.

She pulled the blanket up closer around her. She'd rented this chalet on the mountainside. The pictures of it were the first thing that had attracted her. Whoever had decorated had an eye for detail. The walls were a creamy gray. Dark wood beams stretched across the vaulted ceiling. A river-stone fireplace climbed two stories high, all the way to the ceiling.

It was gorgeous.

And, even better, it wasn't too far from town but close enough that she could see the area's famed lake.

The lake ...

Fog Lake was so enchanting, spooky, and beautiful at the same time.

The body of water stretched from the center of town, nestled between the mountains. Brynlee had seen pictures and knew in the summer that the water could almost look turquoise. But, when the weather was right—more times than not—clouds and mist hung just over the top of the lake, giving it an eerie feel.

Apparently, there were legends that went along with the lake, legends that tied in with the area's Native American history.

Still, she could see why people flooded to the atmospheric town.

Brynlee shivered as she remembered today's events. She'd never imagined how things might turn out. Never. Part of her wanted to pack up and head back to Pennsylvania. Especially after she'd seen those scratch marks on her car.

An animal wouldn't have known that was her SUV. But a man dressed like an animal could have.

She shuddered again.

But if she left now, she'd return home a failure. Her half-brothers already thought she was a failure. The last thing she wanted was to prove they were correct. It was bad enough they disliked her so much.

She frowned at the thought of it.

Her three half-brothers were all cookie-cutter images of each other, it seemed. All good-looking. Had never needed to work a day in their lives.

But Mason, the oldest, really didn't like her. He'd not only given her the cold shoulder, but he'd also encouraged his brothers to do the same.

She couldn't understand why. It wasn't like she'd gone out seeking her father in order to claim his fortune. Rather, her father had found her. He'd invited her into his home.

But Mason only resented her.

It didn't matter. As soon as this trek was over and

Brynlee had done what she needed to do here, she didn't plan on staying in touch with them. There was no reason. No reason to be around people who didn't care for her.

As she stared at the fire, a sudden noise caused her to jerk and tea to splash from the cup on her lap.

She turned toward the large glass door leading outside.

A shadow lingered there.

A shadow that looked exactly like the Skookum that had killed those men.

As the creature's eyes met hers, he lifted an arm. His claws sliced into the screen on her patio door, shredding it.

Brynlee screamed.

She was being hunted, she realized. And the predator chasing her just might win.

7

Boone carefully drew his pool cue back and watched as the eight ball went into the right pocket. He straightened, smiled, and took a grandiose bow.

"Better luck next time," he told everyone around him.

His friends all moaned and stepped back.

Boone had just put this pool table in the basement of his house. He'd bought it before the future of his store was on the rocks, and now he might have to sell it in order to pay his bills. Until then, he'd use it as much as he could.

This house used to belong to his parents, but his mom had abandoned the family several years ago and his dad had died of cancer a couple years ago. Luke had lived here up until he married Harper last month. His sister had also moved out recently, deciding to get her own place, and his younger brother had joined the military.

That left just Boone in this big old house.

He had to admit that the quiet wasn't his favorite thing. But that was his situation right now, like it or not. Life had deviated from the path he'd envisioned for himself, a fact he thought about often.

"So, today was cray-cray, wasn't it?" Chigger said with a shake of his head as he leaned on his pool stick. The man was in his early twenties and about fifty pounds overweight with tan skin and long dark hair that he always pulled into a ponytail. He was always smiling, rarely offended, and had a deep, infectious laugh.

"To say the least." Just the thought of everything that had happened caused Boone's stomach to tighten.

Luke stepped away from the conversation and grabbed a drink from the fridge across the room. His brother didn't usually like to talk shop when he was away from work. Chigger, on the other hand, loved to keep up with town gossip.

"Did I hear the woman say something about an animal beast thing?" Chigger continued.

Boone thought about the conversation. Thought about Brynlee's frantic explanation. Thought about what he'd seen today. "That's what she said."

"What do you think that's about? Do you think it's . . ." He wagged his eyebrows.

"No, Skookums are not real," Boone said. "We all know that. Right, Abe?"

Abe had been Boone's best friend since they were five. He ran a rental company here in town that featured kayaks, climbing equipment, and tubes. The man was short, lean, and had sported the same buzz cut since the fourth grade.

Abe shrugged. "If you talk to my cousin, Fowler, he'll tell you that he's seen him before."

"That's right. There are reports out there, man . . ." Chigger turned away for long enough to grab a potato chip and jam it into some French onion dip.

"Those were bear attacks." Luke popped back into the conversation and took a long sip of his drink.

"But—"

"And all the evidence we found today points to a bear attack," Luke continued. "We have rangers out there now looking for this beast."

"But the woman said she saw—"

"When people are under stress, their minds can play tricks on them," Luke continued, using his professional voice. "That's all it was."

Chigger finally nodded and backed down, but he didn't look convinced. "Okay, if you say so. But I know that the truth is out there."

Boone wadded up a piece of paper that had been left on the counter and threw it at him. "You should join *The X-Files* cast then, conspiracy theorist."

"Hey, one day we're going to discover Bigfoot really exists too."

Boone, Abe, and Luke exchanged a look and a shake of their heads.

As they did, Luke's phone rang. He put it to his ear, and his expression changed from amused to concerned. He lowered his phone and started toward the door, leaving his drink on the counter.

"What is it?"

"That was dispatch. Brynlee Parker said this animal beast thing is outside her chalet right now. I've got to get over there."

Boone grabbed his jacket and started after him. "Mind if I come along?"

"Not as long as you stay out of my way."

Boone looked back at Chigger. "Lock up before you leave, okay?"

"You know it. Go catch that Skookum."

Brynlee stared at the creature at her door and placed the phone back on the cradle. Her hands shook as terror roared to life inside her.

The creature's eyes locked on hers.

Man?

Bear?

Why didn't she know?

Her blood froze as she sensed him watching her every move.

What was happening here?

How had he found her?

She had no idea.

But she had to get as far away from this creature as possible.

Slowly, Brynlee backed toward the staircase. She nearly stumbled over the bottom step.

Adrenaline sprang to life inside her.

She pushed herself back to her feet and darted up the stairs. As she did, a terrible sound filled the air.

The creature . . . he viciously clawed at her windows. Her door. Her house.

Was he trying to get inside?

She had no idea. But she moved even faster.

As the growls and snarls cut through the air, she sprinted into her bedroom and slammed the door. With trembling hands, she clicked the lock behind her.

She kept running until she reached the bathroom. She repeated the process—slamming and locking that door also.

Her eyes darted across the room as fear invaded

her pores. She needed a weapon.

But what?

Working quickly, she grabbed the only thing she could find: the metal curtain rod that stretched across the shower.

She jerked it from the tile surround, let the rings holding the plastic curtain clunk to the floor, and then she held the rod like a bat.

She waited, her heart slamming into her chest.

Her mind raced.

How had that creature found her? Was it because she'd left her backpack on the trail with her ID inside? Or had he somehow been stalking her all day?

Please, help me. Please.

She sucked in a deep breath, trying to control her breathing.

Quiet sounded around her. Was the creature still here?

No sooner did the question enter Brynlee's mind than did an otherworldly screech fill the air again.

The creature. He was still here.

No, not a creature. He was a man dressed as a creature. Brynlee didn't care if no one else believed her. She knew what she'd seen.

Flashbacks of witnessing those two hikers die filled her mind. She squeezed her eyes shut, trying to wish the images away. But it would be a long time before she'd get past the events that had happened today.

Her breath caught as a new sound teased her hearing.

Was that a siren?

Were the cops finally here?

Brynlee prayed that was the case.

Until then, she was staying here. In this room. Behind as many doors as she could.

8

A s a bone-chilling wind blew over the lake, Boone shone his light on the ground outside Brynlee's cabin. He pulled his knit cap lower on his ears.

A cold front had swept through just an hour earlier. A few snowflakes even spit from the sky.

As police lights flashed in the distance, adding their sad blue-and-red glow to the scene, Boone continued to study the muddy ground.

Sure enough, he saw tracks there in the dirt.

"Looks like a bear," Luke said, pausing beside him with a frown.

Boone squatted to examine the tracks better. He couldn't argue with his brother. These did appear to be left by a bear.

"It definitely doesn't look human," Boone finally said.

"We'll take impressions, but my guess is that these prints match the ones at our crime scene."

"Are you going to follow the tracks?"

"Tomorrow morning, I'll send someone. It's too late now. He's probably gotten too far away."

"I agree." Boone glanced into the dark woods in the distance. What if the creature hadn't gotten away? What if it was out there now watching them?

Was it gloating? Or waiting to pounce again when they least expected it?

As he rose, Boone's gaze went to the scratch marks on the side of the house. The marks ripped through the screen door, the window facing, even the log siding.

An animal had definitely been here tonight. A savage animal who seemed to be hunting Brynlee.

Boone glanced inside through the patio doors. Brynlee sat on the couch, a blanket around her shoulders, staring vacantly into the fire. She was definitely traumatized.

Again.

He'd been the one who found her in the bathroom upstairs, holding the metal curtain rod. She'd nearly collapsed with relief when she'd seen him.

He'd checked out the inside of her place but had found nothing.

As much as Boone wanted to stay away from her, he just didn't seem to be able to. Brynlee was so alone right now. Her expensive car, top-of-the-line chalet, and designer clothes didn't afford her any comfort.

The thought caused an unexpected ache in his heart.

"Have you talked to her yet?" Boone asked Luke. He'd seen his brother wander inside while Boone had been searching outdoors.

"Yeah, she's pretty shaken up." Luke glanced at him. "You want to give it a try?"

"Give what a try?"

"Offering some support? You know you have that magical way with people. You always have."

"I don't have a way with this girl. She can't stand me."

Luke shrugged. "You might be surprised. I'm going to set up some lights out here so we can collect evidence. If you wouldn't mind . . ."

"I'm only doing this for you." Boone let out a long breath and stepped toward the door. There was no one else here for her. And a force greater than themselves seemed to throw them together again.

Quietly, he walked toward Brynlee and sat a comfortable distance away on the couch. "Hey."

She barely turned to look at him. "I'm starting to think you're a part of the sheriff's department here."

"I happened to be with Luke when he got the call. I thought he could use a hand. I'm not trying to act like I know what's best for everyone or anything . . ."

Brynlee frowned as more regret filled her gaze. "I shouldn't have said that earlier. I'm sorry."

"I'm just giving you a hard time. Believe me, I wish that was the worst thing people had to say about me." He rubbed his hands on his legs. "How are you doing?"

"I've been better."

"I'm sorry this is happening to you, Brynlee." There. Boone had said it. It was the truth. He *was* sorry this was happening to her. He wished the woman had someone here to offer support during a time like this.

Brynlee said nothing, only stared at the fire.

Boone let her be quiet. Gave her time to process. Stayed where he was in case she wanted to share her thoughts.

Because during the hard times of his life, that's what he'd wanted the most also. Not someone who forced him to talk. But someone who simply stood by him when he needed it the most.

Brynlee couldn't stop thinking about everything that

had happened. Now that Boone sat inside with her, her heart had calmed considerably. Just his presence gave her an unusual comfort, and she was grateful for his quiet.

She needed to contend with her tumultuous thoughts.

How could she stay here in Fog Lake after all this?

But another question remained also: How could she leave?

She stared at the dancing fire in front of her.

She knew the truth. She couldn't leave. But was it worth it to die for her cause?

Think like Dad would, she told herself. *What kind of solution would he find in a moment like this?*

What kind of solution *was* there?

If she stayed here in Fog Lake, she needed to put some precautionary measures in place. She couldn't see herself staying here at the chalet alone after what had happened. Yet would she feel any safer in a hotel? If she moved into town?

She had no idea.

It didn't seem like she'd be safe anywhere. This . . . this *beast* seemed to have finely honed senses that could track her.

She sat up slightly as a new thought hit her. But she could hire someone to protect her. Maybe there was a retired officer here in town.

It was the only solution that made sense.

As Sheriff Wilder came back into the room, Brynlee stood, feeling a new hope sweep through her.

"I need to hire someone to work security for me," she announced. "Is there anyone in town you can recommend?"

Luke remained silent a moment before shrugging. "I agree that having some protection could be wise. There's only one person who comes to mind, really."

"Who's that? I want to see if he's available ASAP."

"You can ask him now." His gaze turned to Boone. "He's sitting right there."

9

Boone felt himself rise up, irritation rushing through him.

"Have you lost your mind?" He stared at his brother, unsure what exactly Luke was thinking. Boone didn't work security. He had no experience. No desire. He ran a camping store for a living.

Luke shrugged, unaffected. "You are the only person who makes sense."

"You can't be serious." Brynlee looked equally as displeased with his suggestion. "He works retail. No offense. But that doesn't exactly make him body-guard material."

"Boone has the best instincts of anyone I know." Luke's voice sounded convincing enough to win the trial of the century. "He was an Eagle Scout, an Army Ranger, *and* he was offered a position with the US

Park Service—a position he turned down. He's a skilled marksman, a survival expert, and he knows this area better than anyone I know. Don't let his unassuming demeanor and boyish good looks fool you."

"I have a store to run." Boone forced his voice to come out in even tones.

"Tourist season doesn't pick up for another three weeks. Chigger can handle it until then." Luke wasn't even playing. No, he was dead serious. His brother had lost his mind.

Boone's scowl deepened. He couldn't believe Luke had put him in this position.

"There's really no one else you can think of?" Brynlee's voice sounded nearly desperate.

Luke's gaze traveled to Deputy Cruise as he poked around outside on the deck, mulling over the evidence there. "He could do it on his off hours."

The deputy dropped his flashlight and fumbled to pick it up from the ground. Boone forced his lips not to curl in a smile. He liked Cruise. He really did. But the man still had a lot to learn about police work.

Boone's gaze went back to Brynlee. She watched Cruise also and frowned.

"Look, I didn't say I was interested in the job, so don't get all stressed out over this." Boone waved his hand in the air in a "don't sweat it" motion.

Brynlee rose and let out a long, resigned breath. "I need someone to watch out for me until I'm finished with my business here. It's not an option for me. If you're the only person here available, then fine. I can pay a thousand a day, and I'll need you for the minimum of one week."

A thousand a day? Man, Boone could use that kind of money. If he worked for Brynlee for even a week, that would be a nice down payment on the repairs he needed to do at his store. Maybe he wouldn't have to choose between selling his family home and his business.

He stared at her another moment.

She was high maintenance. Foolhardy. Too beautiful for her own good.

Working for her would be a challenge.

"It's going to be a little hard for you to pay me considering your checkbook was probably in your backpack." Boone watched her reaction. If he was honest with himself, he might admit he was trying to get a rise out of her.

Brynlee scowled, her luminous brown eyes narrowing with irritation. "I'll make sure you get your money."

Boone chewed on the idea another minute before nodding. He'd been praying that he could find a way to pay his bills. How could he say no now?

"Fine, I can do it." Boone's jaw tightened, and he

hoped he didn't regret his words. "But if you start to do anything stupid—"

"I won't." Her scowl deepened.

He extended his hand. "Then you've got a deal, Ms. Parker."

Brynlee straightened up the chalet, removing any evidence of her ulterior motives for being here in Fog Lake. The last thing she needed was for Boone to get nosy and start asking too many questions. Her goal in coming here was to stay under the radar.

So far, she'd failed.

Sheriff Wilder was staying here with her while Boone ran home to pick up a few things. He'd been on the phone, talking to several people about what sounded like police business. Several times, he referred to his notepad.

At least he was taking this seriously.

Shoving her laptop back into a bag, Brynlee shook her head. She still wasn't sure why she'd agreed to have Boone of all people be her security detail. But in a small town like this, she didn't have many options.

Sheriff Wilder jammed his phone back into his pocket and turned toward her. His expression clearly showed his apprehension, but he offered no new information.

Brynlee paused by the fireplace, reveling in the heat warming her. "Anything I need to know about those marks outside?"

"They appear to match those from the murder scene."

She touched her throat, which suddenly felt dry. "I see. So that man . . . he tracked me back here."

The sheriff frowned and sounded almost compassionate as he said, "By all appearances, it was a bear out there. If it was a man . . . he could have broken a window to get inside or there would be jimmy marks by the door. There was none of that. This has all the signs of a wild animal."

"It was a man." Her jaw tightened. "I know it."

The sheriff lowered himself onto the couch, but his body still looked stiff. "Why would a man go through all the trouble to look like a wild animal?"

She shrugged and remained by the fire. "I have no idea. But a wild animal wouldn't have stolen my backpack either."

Sheriff Wilder nodded slowly, thoughtfully. "There could have been other hikers in the area who came across the bag and took it. The trails are usually safe, but we do on occasion have people who want to go up in the mountains just to get high and cause trouble."

"I'm sorry you don't believe me, but I know what I saw." Brynlee's voice wavered with fear. It would be a long time before she was able to relax. Before she would forget about what she'd experienced so far in her stay here. Maybe she would never forget it.

"I assure you that we're doing everything we can to find answers, Ms. Parker," the sheriff said. "In the meantime, you'll be in good hands. My brother can be a pain, but he's very efficient and capable. I didn't recommend him just because he's family."

"I hope so." She was wagering everything on it. But if what the sheriff had said was true, then she should be fine. A former Army Ranger? Eagle Scout? Survival expert?

She could do far worse.

Just then, Boone appeared at the door with a duffle bag in hand.

She frowned.

Here went nothing.

10

H e watched from his place behind a thick evergreen tree. Saliva pooled at the back of his throat, and hunger made his stomach growl.

He lingered so close, yet no one knew. He mixed in with the darkness, just as he always had. Life had afforded him a natural camouflage that allowed him to blend in effortlessly.

The attribute wasn't physical. Or maybe it was. He didn't know. He only knew that he was practically invisible—at least when he needed to be.

The best part was that no one would suspect he was a killer.

He observed as Boone Wilder lay on the couch in the living room of Brynlee Parker's vacation rental.

Yes, he knew her name. He knew why she was

here too, thanks to that letter in her backpack. Fate had played a role today. He hadn't even known she was an enemy—until a few hours ago.

Boone Wilder? Certainly, Brynlee didn't think he could protect her.

No one could.

Because he knew why she was here.

He hadn't expected to see her on the trail. Somehow his finely tuned instincts had missed her presence. Probably because those two jerks had distracted him. That was okay. He'd taken care of them.

Then he'd chased Brynlee. He feared she'd seen too much.

But the woman had been faster than he thought. His only advantage was that he knew this land. That he took his victims by surprise. But speed? No, he'd never had that.

As Brynlee had reached the camping store, he'd turned. He'd gone back to the spot where she'd been. Had found her bag. Discovered her name.

His fingers dug into the tree bark until the wood wedged beneath his nails. He ignored the pain shooting through him. Ignored the blood that sprouted at his fingertips.

His mission had become to stop Brynlee Parker at all costs.

At all costs?

He shook his head as a new voice began nagging him from a distance. No, not from a distance. It was coming from somewhere in the hollows of his mind.

It was always there, trying to talk to him.

You can't hurt that woman. You don't have to do this. There are other ways.

He shook his head and pressed his hands against his temples.

Yes, you have to. You know what you have to do. People are counting on you.

He pressed his hands harder into the sides of his head.

At all costs. That's right.

He lowered his hands and raised his chin as a moment of peace washed over him. His job was to protect this area from predators. Just as his ancestors had been doing for years before.

He had to do this.

He had to stop Brynlee Parker.

And that meant she had to die.

No voice of reason inside him was going to stop that.

11

———

Boone punched the pillow beneath him and sighed, trying to get comfortable on the couch.

There was a spare bedroom in Brynlee's chalet—three of them, actually—but he felt better sleeping out in the living room where he could keep an eye on things.

He and Brynlee hadn't spoken much after Luke left. Not only was it now the middle of the night and exhaustion had kicked in, but tension crackled in the air between them. She didn't really care for him, and Boone didn't care for her much either.

Maybe Boone should have thought harder before taking this job. It had been a bad, bad idea. Spontaneous. Egged on by the payout.

The money would be an answer to so many of his problems.

Plus, if he were honest with himself, there was a small part of Boone that felt protective of this newcomer in town. Not because he was attracted to Brynlee but because she seemed so alone here.

She'd been through more in the past sixteen hours than most people went through in their lifetime. Seeing those men being killed. The menacing scratches on her SUV. Having a strange creature mark her chalet door.

In the morning, Luke and the park rangers would search these woods, looking for more tracks. They would try to figure out exactly what was going on here.

It hadn't been that long ago that four people had been killed in this area. Boone had hoped that evil had left the area when the man responsible had been arrested.

Then again, this town had always been haunted by some type of generational curse, hadn't it?

Images began to pummel him. Images of Katherine. About how much she loved this area.

She was one of the reasons Boone had decided to stay. When he'd gotten out of the army, the national park service had offered him a job.

But Katherine had loved Fog Lake. She'd wanted to stay here forever and raise a family in a small town—just like she'd been raised. Her whole life revolved around this area.

She worked as a personal trainer here in town. Whenever she hadn't been working, she was organizing 5Ks, planning treks through the mountains, and seeking out new adventures.

She should still be with him now.

Boone's stomach churned at the thought, as it always did.

He blamed himself for her death. If only he'd done things differently that day, Katherine would still be with him now.

That was something he'd never forgive himself for.

He punched his pillow again, desperately wishing for sleep to find him.

He had no such luck.

Instead, it appeared he'd have to contend with his thoughts all night.

Brynlee awoke with a start.

It took a moment for her to remember where she was.

Here in Fog Lake. In the chalet she'd rented. Sleeping under a warm quilt.

Her quick moment of relief disappeared.

In its place were the awful events of yesterday. Seeing those men murdered. Seeing the claw marks on her car. Seeing that beast outside her chalet.

And then there was Boone.

He was here.

Downstairs.

Her unease turned into apprehension.

Brynlee had to get dressed, go downstairs, and remain pleasant. She'd make the best of this business arrangement. She should be used to uncomfortable situations. When she'd been thrust into her father's family, it had been awkward, to say the least. Her three half-brothers didn't exactly welcome her into their brood. They seemed threatened by her instead.

They'd all grown up affluent. Lived a jet-setting lifestyle. And then there was Brynlee, whose mom had lived a gypsy-like existence, unsuccessfully pursuing her passions until the day she'd died. Most of Brynlee's clothes had been secondhand, she'd lived out of an old RV for much of her childhood, and she knew nothing about fancy dinners or cocktail parties.

Not that Boone was like that. But he was off-putting in a different way.

Brynlee didn't know what it was about the man that rubbed her the wrong way, but it was definitely there. Then again, maybe she should be thankful. He was nothing like Will.

At least Boone would be providing a service to her right now. She'd never had to hire security before, and she felt a little silly doing so. But the threat was real. There was no way she could continue staying here in town alone.

She could put up with Boone Wilder if it meant she was safe. Besides, he'd shown a halfway human side when he'd helped her at the camping store after she'd run down the trail.

Still, why did a flutter of nerves rush through her at the thought of seeing him again? It made no sense.

Brynlee went through her morning routine before wandering downstairs. Her gaze went to the couch. It was empty. The blanket had been folded and placed neatly on top of the pillow.

She glanced around. Where had Mr. High and Mighty gone?

She followed the noises into the kitchen and found Boone staring into the refrigerator.

Brynlee paused for a moment to observe him. She loved how manly he was. Loved that he didn't appear to be the type who spent hours in the gym. She guessed that his muscles had been earned from hours of being outside, hiking, rafting, climbing. As

an art major, Brynlee definitely knew about appreci-
ating beauty.

And Boone, physically at least, was a sight to
behold.

"Yogurt and fruit and nuts? Is that all you eat?"
he asked, poking his head out of the refrigerator
long enough to show his frown.

"They're good for you." She squeezed past him
and grabbed a container of Greek yogurt from the
fridge.

"Don't you just want some protein sometimes?"

"You'd be surprised at how much protein this
one little package contains." She pulled a spoon out
of the drawer. "Let me guess. You're a meat and pota-
toes kind of guy."

"Is there any other way to be?"

"Don't get me started." She peeled the silver top
from her container, stared at the creamy blueberry
yogurt inside, then stared at Boone as he closed the
fridge. "How'd you sleep?"

"I didn't." He leaned against the counter and
crossed his muscular arms over his chest. Apparently, he'd given up on finding food.

"I'm sorry to hear that. I didn't sleep either if that
makes you feel any better. I kept . . . listening." An
involuntary shiver raced up her spine.

Brynlee had expected that beast to return. She'd
expected to hear that horrible shriek. To hear his

claws digging into her home. To feel the cold fear that came with knowing something deadly considered her prey.

Thankfully, it hadn't happened.

"What's on your schedule today, Boss?" Boone stared at her, a halfway amused expression on his face.

Something about the way he said that word "Boss" made Brynlee's stomach clench with resentment. Was he mocking her? She brushed it off. "I have to stop by the sheriff's office, for starters."

"Check."

"I also need to see about getting my car back and having a new key made. I'll probably need to pick up a new cell phone."

"Sounds good. As soon as you're done eating, we can get moving."

How was it that Brynlee had hired him, yet he still seemed to be ordering her around?

More irritation pinched at her, and, just to annoy Boone, she took her time eating the rest of her yogurt.

She was in charge, and a bossy outdoorsman wasn't going to convince her otherwise.

12

Boone offered to drive Brynlee to the sheriff's office. As he parked and walked Brynlee toward the station, he called hello to a few people. No doubt more rumors would emerge about him and the mystery woman—especially since they'd been spotted together two days in a row now. Not that Boone cared. He'd lived in the small town for almost his entire life, so he should be used to the gossip in a place so close-knit.

As Brynlee stepped inside to give her statement to Luke, Boone grabbed a donut from the breakroom and then stepped outside to make a phone call to Chigger.

"Hey, I need you to supervise the store today. You think you can handle that?"

"I think so. But you should know, there were

some big rocks, some new ones, in the stream down from the store this morning."

Boone's spine stiffened. "Really? How many?"

"Hard to say. Maybe six or seven. They were pretty big. The mountainside is becoming more unstable."

Great. That was the last thing Boone wanted to hear right now. He'd hoped the earlier incidents were just flukes, but no such luck.

"What do you have going on?" Chigger asked. "Does it have to do with LL Bean?"

Boone's stomach clenched. "Maybe—but it's not like you think."

Chigger let out a low whistle that implied there was more to this arrangement than there was. "She's a pretty thing."

Boone scowled. "I'm working for her. You know me. I'm not looking for any kind of relationship. Not a fling, not a long-term something. Nothing."

"Okay, man, okay. Didn't mean to push your buttons. I'll keep a watch on things. You can count on me."

Last time Boone had counted on him to watch his store for a significant amount of time, Chigger had managed to unplug the refrigerator and all the bait went bad. In the process, the entire store had reeked for the next week.

"Let me know if any hikers come in and mention anything strange out there on the trails, okay?"

"You got it."

Boone ended his call and stepped back inside, toward Luke's office. He got there just in time to see Luke raise something up from the floor behind his desk. "And look what someone turned in this morning."

Brynlee's eyes widened. "My backpack."

"Unfortunately, your wallet is gone. But at least you can rest assured that whoever killed those two men didn't take your bag."

Brynlee looked through it, almost frantically. When she stopped, her face paled.

"What's wrong?" Boone asked. "What are you missing?"

She looked up, her eyes wide with surprise "Nothing. I mean . . . just my wallet. My father's ashes, my phone, and my keys are here. That's an answered prayer."

"You might want to cancel your credit cards and report your driver's license as stolen to the DMV."

"Good idea."

"And you said you'll be in town for the next week in case we have any questions?" Luke continued.

"Yes, sir." Brynlee glanced at Boone then back at Sheriff Wilder. "I'm going to start calling some of those companies right now before my credit cards get charged up."

"Feel free to use the conference room down the hall."

"Thanks."

As she disappeared, Boone stepped into Luke's office. "How's it going?"

"Not much sleep last night and not many answers yet." Luke looked tired. This case was already taking a toll on him. With such a small department, a crime like this would easily consume the staff on hand.

Boone sat down across from him. "Did they identify those two bodies yet?"

"They were college kids from up in Michigan, here on their spring break. Their IDs were still on them when we recovered their bodies."

"Interesting."

"We also had two witnesses come forward and tell us they saw Ms. Parker talking to these men the day before."

Boone's back muscles tightened. "What? She didn't mention that."

Luke's stern look made it clear he shared the thought. "Apparently, they were hitting on her. Being pretty obnoxious. She told them to get lost."

"Does that play into this investigation?" Boone

waited, holding his breath as he waited for Luke's conclusion.

"It means we keep an eye on her. She had a bad encounter with those men, and then they ended up dead, and she was the one who reported the incident."

There had been some friction between Boone and Brynlee, but he couldn't see the woman being a killer. Besides, how would she make it look like a bear attack? It wouldn't make sense. Plus, she'd been so frightened from witnessing it.

But Boone understood that his brother had to consider all the options.

Boone cleared his throat, trying to keep his thoughts focused. "What's next?"

"Next, I get to call their parents. The medical examiner is still doing the autopsy."

"Do their deaths appear to be from a bear attack?"

"It does. The tracks make it look like a big one. Probably five or six hundred pounds."

"What would make a bear do something like that?"

"Who knows? Maybe it was hungry or rabid or provoked. It's hard to say. We've put out a warning to anyone who's thinking about hiking, though. They need to be on guard until this creature is captured."

Boone shook his head. "A bear attack, huh? It's

been four years since we've had one of those around here."

Luke frowned. "I know. And with tourist season coming up, this isn't good."

"I heard Jason Sawyer with the park service and Abe have been tracking the bear."

"That's right."

"Hopefully, they'll catch this creature and everyone's fears will be put to rest."

"Let's hope."

An incident like this wouldn't affect just Luke. No, it would affect the whole town. If too many people were scared away, it could even harm their livelihood here.

That meant there was a lot riding on finding answers.

Brynlee paused outside Sheriff Wilder's office. She'd come back to ask the man a question, though she'd forgotten what it was now.

She got to the door just in time to overhear the last part of the conversation.

A bear. Everyone was still convinced an animal had done this.

What if she was wrong and they were right? What if, in her stress, her eyes had deceived her?

Brynlee looked up as a man approached from the lobby. The older gentleman offered an affable smile before raising his hand to knock at Luke's office. The man had thin white hair, he was tall and lanky, and had a grandfatherly vibe about him.

"I hope I'm not interrupting," he said.

"Not at all." Brynlee stepped back, her cheeks heated. She'd so clearly been eavesdropping that she couldn't even deny it.

"Sheriff Wilder, it's Lonny Thompson with Fish and Wildlife. I heard you had some questions about yesterday's attack."

"Lonny, yes, thanks for coming." The sheriff's voice rang into the hallway. "Come on in. I have a few questions for you." His eyes shifted to Brynlee. "You can come in also. Maybe you can add some insight into this."

With some hesitation, Brynlee stepped into the room and stood quietly. Boone was also inside, leaning casually against the wall with his arms crossed, looking as if he had all the time in the world. For a moment, she envied how laid-back he looked.

"Lonny is a bear expert, and we've asked him to come here to help us identify if a bear was involved in this attack. Later, he's going to examine the bodies —the claw marks. Saliva. He'll look at the bear tracks. But I wanted to get his insight into the situation."

The sheriff ran over the account with the man, who listened intently. Luke then pulled out some of the crime scene photos, showing the claw marks and footprints.

Lonny examined them for several minutes, asked some questions, and then lowered the photos back onto Luke's desk.

"It clearly sounds like a bear was behind these attacks," Lonny said. "That's what all the evidence points to. So why is this even a question?"

Luke pointed to her. "Brynlee, why don't you tell him what you saw?"

"I saw . . ." She fumbled for her words a moment. "At first, I thought it was a bear attack. I mean, this . . . this . . . thing moved differently than I thought that a bear might, but I've never seen a bear in real life either. But as the second man was attacked, this creature stood up on his hind legs. When I saw his face . . . it almost looked human."

"So, it didn't have a snout or black eyes?"

"No, it did." Brynlee shook her head. "But it was almost like that head was covering a . . . a human head."

Saying it out loud, she knew she sounded foolish. But she told the truth.

"Throughout history, there have been times

when bears have been mistaken for humans or even for Bigfoot," Lonny said. "Bears have an interesting bipedal gait they use to walk upright sometimes, giving them an appearance of almost being human. There are numerous reported cases of this happening."

Brynlee bit back a frown. What if everyone was right? What if she was reading too much into this?

No, she had to stick to her guns. Besides, there were other things that weren't so easily explained . . . "But, if that's true, then what about the bear that came to my place last night? Was that just a coincidence?"

"It's not uncommon for bears to sometimes get nosy. It's a little early in the year for them to be coming out now. But it's entirely possible."

"I have a hard time believing I'd have encounters with two separate bears."

"I also feel like it's unlikely," Lonny said. "But I've seen stranger things happen."

Brynlee held back a frown.

This wasn't what she wanted to hear . . . but maybe it was what she *needed* to hear. Maybe she should listen to these people who were more objective about this situation. Because her emotions were telling her there was more to this story than anyone else wanted to believe.

Boone's heart twisted when he saw the disappointment on Brynlee's face. She really was honestly having a hard time believing this could be a bear. Sometimes the truth was hard to accept.

For a moment, he was tempted to reach out to her. To try to make her feel better. To offer a shoulder to lean on.

But he didn't.

Boone had been hired to protect her physically, not to guard Brynlee's heart.

Instead, he stood, thanked Luke and Lonny, and met her in the hallway. "Did you get those cards canceled?"

She pushed a hair back from her face. "No, I didn't. I came to ask a question."

"What question would that be?"

"My SUV . . . can we pick it up sometime soon?"

"Absolutely." Boone kept a hand on her elbow and led her back down to the conference room. "You get your cards cancelled before you regret it. You don't need financial problems on top of everything else, right?"

She nodded stiffly, still looking flustered. "Yes, of course."

"Do you need me to help you?"

"I think I've got it. I saved my card numbers on my phone, so I just need to call."

"I'm here if you need me."

Brynlee looked up at him, the first touch of gratefulness in her eyes. "Thank you."

Before Boone could say anything else, his phone rang. He glanced at the screen and saw that it was Witherford Johnson, a friend who worked for the city. He and Boone were on the Planning Council together.

He excused himself and answered. "Hey, Witherford. What's going on?"

"Hey, Boone. I just found out something I thought you should know. Someone has submitted a commercial zoning permit for Dead Man's Bluff."

"What? What do you mean?" He held his breath, waiting for his response.

"As you know, the land is privately owned. Well, the owner wants to build a resort up there."

"Who? Who's behind this?" About ten years ago, someone affiliated with the owner had come into town, wanting to develop the mountain. Thankfully, he'd been shot down.

"A company called Brinkley and Sons. Ever heard of them?"

"Aren't they the same company who filed several years ago?" The name was familiar. If he remembered correctly, Tom Brinkley was a developer who'd opened several resorts across the country.

"Yes, Brinkley and Sons have tried this before. They own the land, but without the right permits, they won't be able to get the infrastructure up there to support something like this. We can make sure of that."

Boone's heart lifted. "So it's been blocked?"

"Not officially. We're looking for legal loopholes that will make this null and void before the process even starts."

"Good. I hope you find them. I mean, it's not really a possibility that this can happen, is it?" The area was special, even more so because Katherine had loved it so much. Because of that, Boone felt fiercely protective of the mountain.

"I mean, it is private land. And it was, at one time, zoned for commercial use. Last time, we had protests to demonstrate our displeasure at the proposal. Our message came across loud and clear. Anyway, I thought you'd want to know since . . . well, you know."

"Yes, thanks. Please keep me updated. A resort is the last thing this town needs."

Suddenly, Boone's bad day felt even worse. He took a few deep breaths. He would take this one step at a time . . . but no way would he let the area around Dead Man's Bluff be developed . . . he would do everything in his power to stop it.

As they walked back out to Boone's truck, his phone rang again. Brynlee tried to mind her own business as she reviewed what she needed to get done. The important thing was that she'd been able to cancel her cards. The bad news was that it would take two days to get her new ones in the mail. She'd had them sent to her chalet address. Until then, she was going to have to get by with only thirty-three dollars to her name.

The other bad news was that her papers were gone. The ones that she'd had a lawyer draw up. The ones that would make it clear to anyone who found them why she was here.

Her stomach twisted at the thought. Why would

someone take those papers? What would they do with that information?

It just didn't make any sense. Her dad had warned her that she would have opposition. That she'd make enemies. That the town wouldn't welcome her.

But . . . things weren't supposed to go like this.

As Boone grinned and spoke into the phone, Brynlee's curiosity spiked. She listened to the one-sided conversation, wondering who he was speaking with.

"Oh, Ansley," he said with a grunt. "I'm sorry. I totally forgot about lunch today. Something's come up."

Ansley? Was she a girlfriend? Brynlee hadn't given much thought to how Boone's girlfriend might feel about him acting as bodyguard for another woman. She hoped she hadn't put him in an awkward situation.

"I know, I know. You know you're important to me," Boone continued as they climbed into his truck.

Brynlee's heart lurched again as she realized the trouble she could be causing for him. She hadn't really thought everything through before hiring him.

Brynlee would probably be okay by herself during daylight hours, especially if she stayed in town. It was only when she went near the woods that trouble seemed to be drawn to her. As much as she longed for security right now, maybe it was better if she let Boone off the line for now.

Brynlee motioned toward him and mouthed, "Don't cancel on my account."

Boone paused and craned his neck toward her before looking back through the windshield.

She could hear the other woman—Ansley— talking through the phone line, though she couldn't make out any words. The woman definitely sounded animated, though. High maintenance? That's what Brynlee would guess.

"Okay, okay." Boone's voice turned placating. "Wait just a minute. Maybe I *can* meet you. You mind if I bring someone with me?"

Oh, great. He was going to bring Brynlee to meet his girlfriend? This was going to be awkward, not to mention unnecessary.

He said a few more things into the phone before ending the call and looking back at Brynlee.

"You sure you don't mind?" he clarified.

"Not at all. I know our arrangement was all last minute."

Boone put his phone on his dashboard and cranked the engine. "If you don't mind then I think I will keep this lunch date. It's kind of important to me. It's been longstanding for the past three years. Every Tuesday."

That sounded nice—having someone that stable in your life. That kind of consistency was something Brynlee had never had.

"Please don't let me keep you from it then. But you don't have to bring me along. I'm sure you want privacy."

"Oh, you should meet Ansley. I think you'll like her." Boone flashed a smile that sent Brynlee's nerves shooting through the roof.

"Great." But her voice sounded unconvinced.

A few minutes later, they pulled up in front of the Hometown Diner, he parked, and they stepped outside.

Brynlee froze there on the sidewalk and grabbed Boone's arm. "Look at that."

He followed her gaze and, with confusion in his voice, asked, "What am I looking at?"

"That view." She stared at the mountains in the distance. Fog cloaked the peaks, and the whole scene reflected on the lake below. She'd never seen anything like it. "It's breathtaking."

Boone smiled at her. "Yes, it is, isn't it?"

"I can see why my parents liked it here."

He raised his brow. "Your parents?"

Brynlee nodded. "They came here on one of their first dates. My dad said this place was magical."

"I'd agree. There's no place like Fog Lake." Boone put his hand on her back and directed her away.

His touch jolted her, but Brynlee ignored the feeling. She tried to, at least.

"Come on. Let's get inside. I'd hate to be late and face the wrath of Ansley."

But as they turned, Brynlee nearly stumbled into a man who stood behind them. She hadn't even heard him approach.

Her gaze traveled down to his chest, and she saw his necklace.

It was a gigantic bear claw.

Brynlee sucked in a breath as her eyes fluttered to the man's face. A hostile look stained his eyes.

Terror coursed through her. Was this the man Brynlee had seen murder those two college boys on the trail? Why else would he be staring at her with such malice?

14

Boone ushered Brynlee away from the man and inside the warm restaurant that smelled like childhood outings with her mom. Oldies music blared overhead, and the place looked surprisingly full.

"It's okay," Boone muttered to Brynlee as he shut the door behind them. "He's harmless."

"That man didn't seem harmless." She remembered his face. His leathery skin. The scar on his cheek. His silent stare.

"He's . . . well, he's a bit of a fixture around here. We call him Big Ben."

"What do you know about him?" Brynlee made no effort to move from the entrance.

"He never talks, for starters. He's lived here for

nearly as long as I can remember, and I've never heard him say a word."

"How does he work and support himself?"

Boone shrugged. "I'm not 100 percent sure. I think he owns a small cabin up in the mountains. Maybe it was passed on to him by his family. The last I heard, he was making baskets and selling them on the side of the road."

Brynlee remembered the look in the man's eyes. She remembered . . . "That bear claw . . . around his neck . . ."

"I know." Boone's jaw tightened.

He was worried too, wasn't he? But he didn't want to admit it to her. Was this man connected with the crime she'd seen?

Before they could talk about it anymore, Boone's gaze met someone's in the distance, and he ushered Brynlee in that direction.

Brynlee watched as Boone kissed the cheek of the pretty woman who waited for him in the corner booth.

Ansley looked a little wilder than someone Brynlee had expected Boone to date—not that she knew that much about the man. She'd just pictured him with someone more natural looking, she supposed. Someone outdoorsy but pretty and athletic.

This woman—Ansley—had bleached blonde

hair down to her shoulders, multiple earrings, and even a tattoo peeking out from her sleeve. Her eyes sparkled, and her tight jeans accentuated her killer body. She seemed like a firecracker, the type who could handle anything life threw at her. At least, she did based on first impressions.

"Ansley, this is Brynlee," Boone said, extending his hand toward her. "Brynlee, Ansley."

"I'm sorry to impose on your lunch." Brynlee's throat squeezed with regret.

"It's no problem," Ansley said. "It's always good to see a new face. Have a seat."

Brynlee lowered herself at the end of the table while Boone and Ansley sat across from each other. She shifted, realizing she should have refused to come. Not even John Denver playing on the jukebox made her feel any better.

This was not how she'd envisioned her trip going.

"So, how do you two know each other?" Ansley asked, glancing down at the menu before looking back and forth between them.

Boone hesitated, probably feeling awkward as he tried to answer. Brynlee had put him in this situation. The least she could do was try to smooth it over.

"I hired him to act as private security for me," Brynlee finally said. "I hope that's not weird for you."

Ansley raised her thin eyebrows. "Weird for me? Oh, no. That's not weird at all. At least he's making himself useful. Finally."

Boone gave her a look. "Ha ha. Very funny."

"Just saying . . ."

"You're always just saying." Boone gave Ansley a pointed look.

Brynlee glanced down at her menu, feeling like she was in the middle of something. The two were playful, but the vibes she got from them . . . weren't what she'd expected.

"I'd get the corned beef," Ansley told her. "It's delicious."

"I don't eat meat."

"Then the tomato soup is really good."

Brynlee closed her menu. "Fine. It's settled then."

It was one less decision she'd have to make.

Boone's phone rang, and he stood, excusing himself. "It's Abe. Let me see what's up. I think he has a group that wants to go kayaking next weekend and needs extra equipment."

Brynlee watched as he walked away, calling hello to several people as he did.

Then the awkwardness set in. She wasn't sure what exactly to say to Ansley, and she halfway feared an ugly confrontation.

"Listen, I really do feel like I'm interrupting

something here." Brynlee decided to be direct. "When I hired Boone, it was on a purely professional level."

Ansley stared at her. "Professional or not, it doesn't bother me either way."

"It doesn't?" Ansley was entirely more laid-back than Brynlee would be in a situation like this.

Ansley tilted her head. "Why should it? My brother can do what he wants."

The air left Brynlee's lungs. "Your brother?" Had she heard correctly?

"Yes, my brother. Wait, he didn't tell you that?" Ansley's eyes crinkled with humor.

Brynlee's jaw locked in irritation as she realized all her worry had been for nothing. "No, he didn't."

"Oh, he's messing with you then. I would give him a big old whooping if I were you. He likes to do that sometimes. Play games with people. Messing with people's heads—in a fun-loving way, of course."

Brynlee glanced behind her at Boone. He talked on the phone while still waving at people. The man should be a politician.

Ansley followed her gaze. "It's a shame everything that's happened. He loves this town, and he's a good man."

"Everything that's happened?" Brynlee asked, a new round of curiosity surging to life inside her.

Ansley pushed her eyebrows together. "He didn't tell you?"

"Tell me what?"

Ansley leaned back and shrugged, as if trying to brush it off. "It's nothing."

"It doesn't sound like nothing." What exactly was Boone Wilder's story?

"He'll tell you when he wants to. Until then, just know you can trust him, okay?"

Brynlee nodded but didn't feel as reassured as she would like. Maybe she just needed a moment to compose herself. "I think I'm going to run to the restroom. Please, excuse me."

She hurried to the back of the building. But as Brynlee stepped into the restroom, she nearly collided with an older woman who was leaving.

Brynlee tried to brush past her, but the woman blocked her until she was forced to make eye contact.

"You better hope Boone Wilder doesn't do to you what he did to Katherine," the woman growled, her voice a hoarse whisper. "I'd be careful if I were you."

"What?" Brynlee gasped, certain she hadn't heard correctly. "Who's Katherine?"

The woman didn't say anything. Her glimmering eyes stayed on Brynlee's a moment longer. Then she stepped out of the bathroom, leaving Brynlee with more questions than answers.

Boone observed Brynlee out of the corner of his eye.

Why did she seem shaken? Had something happened on her short walk to the bathroom? What could have possibly taken place?

He shoved the feeling down, figuring it would come up later.

Their food was here, and they all dug in. Not surprising, the donut he'd had for breakfast hadn't held him over. But his burger and fries would.

"So, I heard there was another bear attack," Ansley said, shoving a crispy french fry into some ranch dressing and sounding casual.

"Another one?" Brynlee's voice rang with surprise. "Do they happen a lot in this area?"

"We had some bear attacks about four years ago," Boone explained. "Two people were killed up in the mountains. Hikers."

"And there were the bear attacks ten years ago," Ansley added, waving a french fry at her brother. "Don't forget about them."

"I had no idea there were so many in this area," Brynlee said. "I didn't think they were that common."

"There really haven't been," Boone said. "It just sounds like a lot."

The last thing he needed was for Brynlee to freak

out. Maybe he should have given Ansley a head's up about what had happened to Brynlee yesterday. He'd had no time to talk to her privately.

Brynlee's hands shook so badly at the moment that her tomato soup sloshed from her spoon.

Ansley seemed to notice at the same time Boone did.

"Oh my goodness." Ansley's voice dropped with surprise. "You were the one who was out there when those two men died, weren't you?"

Brynlee swallowed hard and lowered her spoon back into the bowl. She licked her lips, but no words escaped.

"She was," Boone answered for her, a surge of compassion rising in him.

"Man, I can't imagine. I'm so sorry. I wouldn't have brought it up if I'd known."

"It's okay." Brynlee put her spoon down. "It's still just . . . shocking."

"I can imagine. It's been all the buzz around town today. No one can believe it."

"Don't say it," Boone said, anticipating the next words out of his sister's mouth. His shoulders tensed as he waited for the inevitable.

"What?" Brynlee's eyebrows scrunched together in confusion as she peered at them.

"It was the Skookum, wasn't it?" Ansley's eyes widened, her horror turning into fascination.

Boone shook his head. Ansley had done it anyway. Of course.

"It wasn't the Skookum," he muttered.

"Why do people keep bringing the Skookum up?" Brynlee asked. "Do people really believe this thing exists?"

Boone started to answer, but Ansley beat him to it. "Absolutely. There's a lot of folklore around this area. You know about the Native Americans—"

"And the massacre that occurred here," Brynlee finished.

"Yes. Right here in this area. It's crazy to think about how many people lost their lives right here on this very land. It makes up the history of this place. The fiber of it. There's blood in this dirt and tragedy all around us. Nature knows it."

"That's a little dramatic, Ansley." Boone resisted an eye roll.

Ansley leaned back, making it clear she didn't care what anyone else thought. She never had. "But it's the truth. Maybe this town really is haunted."

"I hear you," Boone said.

"You should talk to Fowler," Ansley continued. "He could tell you some stories."

"Fowler?"

"He works for Boone's best friend, Abe. He's a local Skookum expert. He thinks a Skookum killed his dad. Now he's an unofficial authority in the area."

"Good to know," Brynlee said.

Before Boone could argue with her anymore, his phone rang again. It was Chigger.

"You need to get to the store. Pronto. The county inspector is here and asking questions."

Boone frowned and glanced at Brynlee. She was about to discover that he was a terrible person to hire to handle her security. He had too much going on in his own life . . . things that he wished would disappear.

15

Brynlee stared at Boone, trying to figure out what his conversation was about. Had he heard something else about the murder yesterday? Whatever it was, it looked like bad news.

He put his phone away and frowned at Ansley then Brynlee. "Listen, I'm sorry to do this. But I need to stop by my store. It's an emergency."

"Do what you have to do." Brynlee bit back her disappointment.

His store? She'd been selfishly hoping the phone call would provide some answers for herself. When she realized the frustration in her voice had been too apparent, she cleared her throat, determined to cover it up.

"Although, I am starting to think you should be

paying me to tag along with you," she finally said, keeping her voice light.

He frowned and pulled out his wallet. "You're probably right."

Brynlee shrugged. "My hourly pay might be more than yours."

Ansley laughed. "I like this woman."

"That doesn't surprise me." Boone dropped some cash on the table. "Lunch is on me."

"Hope everything works out, bro," Ansley said.

What did that mean? Was Boone having trouble with his store? There was so much Brynlee didn't know. So much she was curious about.

A few minutes later, they were in his truck and headed into the mountains. She tried to relax as Boone drove. She thought about the camping store. The log-sided building was nestled near the mountain. A small creek rippled behind it, and a little water wheel turned at the side of the building, near part of the creek that swept under the roadway.

The building was rustic with a porch and rocking chairs. The inside had been simple yet screamed of every kind of adventure imaginable.

The whole place fit Boone.

The farther away they got from town, the more Brynlee's throat tightened. She wanted to enjoy this area. She really did. But the memories made it hard.

And what about that woman in the bathroom?

Who was Katherine? Why had the woman warned Brynlee about Boone?

The thoughts churned inside her.

What if this Boone guy wasn't as trustworthy as the sheriff made it seem? Sure, he seemed laid-back and friendly, but . . . people could hide dark sides. Brynlee couldn't afford to be naïve here.

"You have something on your mind?" Boone tapped his fingers on the steering wheel.

Brynlee shrugged, wondering whether or not she should bring it up. Then again, how could she hire someone not knowing if she could trust him?

She cleared her throat and tried to sound casual as she asked, "Who's Katherine?"

His eyes widened and his voice rose with surprise. "Katherine? Where did you hear her name?"

Tension embedded itself between her shoulders as she sensed Boone's emotions rising. "A woman stopped me in the bathroom. Told me she hoped you didn't do to me what you did to Katherine."

His face tightened even more. "Nancy . . ." he muttered. "I thought I saw her leaving out the back. I should have known."

"Who's Nancy? Who's Katherine, for that matter?"

Boone shook his head, and his jaw tightened as

he stared at the road in front of them. "It's a long story, far more than I can tell you on this drive."

That wasn't going to work. Kat's mother, Nancy, had practically accused Boone of being a criminal. How could Brynlee trust him if she knew so little about his past?

"You're going to need to tell me soon," Brynlee said. "Because I'm having second thoughts about hiring you. Is there a reason I should be concerned?"

Boone pulled to a stop in front of his store, hitting the brakes harder than she'd anticipated. She lurched forward in the seat.

"If you don't trust me, then feel free to find someone else to act as security for you. But hiring me doesn't mean you're privy to all my business."

A frigid chill filled the air.

Ouch. Brynlee had touched a nerve. But why?

Before she could say anything else, Boone threw the truck into Park and opened the door. Without another word, he stormed into his store.

What had just happened?

Boone's stormy attitude surged to a new level. It was bad enough that Todd Michaels had stopped by his store unannounced. But now Nancy was going around telling Brynlee about Katherine?

When would Katherine's family ever accept the truth?

He didn't have time to think about it right now.

No, Boone had bigger problems—like keeping his store open. He wasn't going to let the county inspector change any of that.

"Mr. Wilder." Todd smiled as he stood near the checkout counter. The small, bald man had exaggerated features and expressions. Everything about him got on Boone's last nerve.

Chigger stood by the register, clicking and unclicking his pen—probably just to annoy Todd.

"Todd." Boone paused and rested his hands on his hips, reminding himself to act professional. "What a surprise."

The man smiled again, the expression smug. "I came to see how the safety improvements were coming."

Boone's jaw tightened. "Haven't started implementing them yet."

"Things are going to get busy real soon. I'd hate to see you shut down right before tourist season gets underway. I can only imagine the money you'd lose."

"I told you we're working on the changes. It takes time."

"This place is a safety hazard, unfit for the public. It should already be shut down."

Boone sensed a shadow behind him and knew

that Brynlee had followed him inside and was listening to this conversation. She was the last person he wanted here right now, though he did regret snapping at her earlier. She couldn't have known what she was bringing up. But he'd told the truth—he didn't owe her an explanation.

"We're going to get this done," Boone said. "You don't have to follow up with us."

"That's my job." Todd raised his pointy little chin.

"Don't you have other business owners to badger?"

Todd smiled, still looking smug. "You're my favorite."

Boone fisted his hands, trying to remain in control. He counted to three. Then counted to three again. And again.

He and Todd had gone to high school together. Todd had liked Katherine and had never forgiven Boone when she'd chosen him over Todd.

Todd pulled something from his briefcase and slapped it on the counter. "I'll be going now. Have a great day. I'll be back to check on things again soon."

The man nodded at Brynlee as he breezed out the door.

A moment of uncomfortable silence fell in the store.

After a moment, Boone grabbed the paper from

the counter and stormed toward his office. He sat at the chair there and read the notice.

He had thirty days to get the changes done or the county was going to condemn this building.

Great.

Where was Boone going to get twenty thousand dollars for these improvements before then?

He knew the answer. He wasn't. Though he wasn't one to give up, that amount was just too much. He'd already applied for a loan and had been denied.

The civil lawsuit had eaten into too much of his savings and had left him nearly broke. Kat's family had taken him to court under wrongful death charges. Everyone in town had seemed to take sides, but, in the end, the judge had ruled in his favor. Still, it had been taxing in more than one way. Thankfully, his family home was in Luke's name, so Nancy and her husband hadn't been able to take that away.

A knock sounded at his door, and Boone looked up to see Brynlee standing there with a sympathetic frown on her face.

"Everything okay?" she asked softly.

"Yeah, I'll be okay." He tried to shake the dark cloud over him, but he couldn't. He always believed in having a backup plan. But right now, he had nothing.

She lowered herself into the seat across from him. "You don't look okay."

"It's just business." Boone thought she would leave. Would see this disaster and flee. Instead, she seemed to be settling in.

"Yeah, I know about that."

He raised an eyebrow. "What exactly do you do for a living?"

"I own my own interior design company."

Boone could see her in that line of work. She seemed trendy and perky enough for the job. Plus, she dressed like someone who appreciated detail and making things look nice. "I see."

"I know all about the struggle of money being tight and fearing you won't be able to pay employees or make ends meet."

He resisted a skeptical grunt. "You don't seem like the type who's struggled."

No, Brynlee seemed like someone who'd had things handed to her. Boone couldn't relate. He liked working hard for what he had. It was the way his dad had taught him.

Brynlee shrugged, a slight defensiveness materializing as she lifted her chin. "You might be surprised. I have my own business, and money is often tight. I suppose I could make more if I focused on high-end clients. But I decided to focus on people who have small budgets instead. We go shopping at thrift stores and estate sales and yard sales to find things to help us decorate."

"That's . . . not what I expected."

"That's only because you made assumptions."

That still didn't explain her expensive car or accommodations. But those things weren't his business, he supposed.

Before he could retort, a loud thump sounded outside.

Boone froze, listening for another signal to what was happening. The next moment, he heard a moan.

Boone turned toward Brynlee, his muscles ready to spring into action. "Where's Chigger? Do you know?"

"He went to take some trash out."

Something was wrong, Boone realized. Those sounds were not normal.

"Stay here," he barked.

And then he took off toward the back.

16

Boone charged out the back door, unsure what he would find. He only knew that his gut told him something bad had happened.

He stopped just outside the door and glanced around. The creek trickled by. The water wheel churned in its flow. A deer scampered away on the mountainside.

He looked for fallen rocks but saw nothing.

A moan sounded in the distance.

Boone darted around the corner and spotted Chigger. His employee was sprawled on the ground there, and his normally tan skin looked pale.

"Chigger." Boone knelt beside him and squinted, looking for injuries. He saw none. "What happened?"

Chigger moaned and touched the back of his head as he tried to sit up. "Skookum . . ."

"What?" Was the man delirious? Boone glanced around, looking again for a sign of anything—or anyone—out of place. "Where did this person go?"

Chigger moaned and shrugged, his gaze not quite coming into focus still. "He hit me . . . and everything went black."

Boone rose. The hair on his arms stood as he scanned the landscape around him again.

Whoever had done this was still around here.

Was close.

He sucked in a deep breath at the realization.

But where had this person gone?

He scanned the wooded mountainside, looking for any type of clue. He saw no one. Nothing.

The man couldn't have gotten but so far away.

Brynlee, Boone realized. What if this person had used Chigger as a distraction and had gone inside to Brynlee? Concern surged in him.

"You'll be okay a minute here by yourself?" Boone asked Chigger.

Chigger nodded, still squinting with discomfort. "Yeah, man."

"I'll be right back." Boone darted back to the store, hoping he wasn't too late.

But, before he rounded the corner, he heard the

back door slam shut. As he reached it, he grabbed the handle.

It was locked.

Someone had locked themselves inside with Brynlee, Boone realized.

He had to figure out how to get through the door. There was no time to waste.

As Brynlee heard the slam in the distance, she stood and rested her hand at her throat.

What had happened out there?

Based on Boone's reaction as he'd darted from the office, something bad.

She backed up until she hit the wall, fear suddenly coursing through her. The emotion had become a familiar companion over the past twenty-four hours.

Who was out there? Was it the same beast who had killed those men?

She knew the answer was most likely yes.

A footfall sounded in the hallway—quiet, timid almost.

That wasn't Boone. Boone would come thundering back in here.

Someone else was in the store, she realized. She sucked in a quick breath.

She glanced around. Was there anything in here she could defend herself with?

She saw an outstanding volunteer award. A picture of Boone beside a pretty woman with wheat-colored hair. A deer head with a hunting cap perched on top.

None of those things would work as weapons.

She shifted her gaze upward. A small window stretched at the top of the wall, but Brynlee couldn't reach it. Even if she could, she wasn't sure she could fit through it.

Another footfall.

Someone was definitely in this store. Someone who wanted to remain stealthy and quiet.

Another vision of a wild beast hunting its prey filled Brynlee's thoughts.

She was being stalked, wasn't she?

And she had no idea what to do about it.

Whoever was out there was getting closer. He would be at the door any minute. She felt certain of it.

"Brynlee!" someone outside yelled. The voice sounded like it came from below the window.

Boone. Why was he yelling from outside?

Had he been locked out? What was going on?

She wanted to answer back. Yet she feared giving away her location. Her throat seemed to seize up on her.

Maybe she should be brave. Maybe she should face this thing head on.

But her body didn't cooperate. She was frozen where she was. Dread dripped in her gut until she thought she would throw up.

A scratching sound sent a shiver up her spine.

The beast was in here. In the store. On the other side of the door.

And he teased her. He wanted to feel her fear, didn't he?

She listened again.

And then nothing.

It was quiet.

Was he gone?

Or was he waiting?

And where was Boone?

Another loud bang cut through the air.

It sounded close. Too close.

Brynlee's heart rate ratcheted again. What if this beast had found a key to the office? Or figured out another way to get her?

The next thing she knew the door to the office flew open.

She braced herself for whatever terror she was about to face.

17

Boone let out a sigh of relief when he spotted Brynlee still in his office. She stood frozen against the wall, a chair pushed in front of her and fear filling her eyes.

His relief was short-lived.

Someone had been in his store. Had locked the doors. Boone had used his shoulder to burst through the back door and get inside.

The question was: Where was this person now? He hadn't escaped out the back door. Did that mean he was still in here somewhere?

"Stay behind me," Boone ordered.

Brynlee didn't argue. In three seconds flat, she was near him. Holding his arm. Close enough that he could feel her body heat.

He drew the gun from his waistband and started through the store.

Five aisles of products stared back at him.

The intruder could be behind any of them, just waiting for the right moment to pounce.

He heard Brynlee's short breaths behind him. The woman was terrified, and rightfully so. Her life was on the line.

Slowly, Boone moved forward. He started by the front door. Scanned the aisle.

Nothing.

He moved on to the next. Then the next. And the next.

Nothing.

"He must be gone," Boone muttered. "Maybe he went out the front door when I came in the back."

"Who? Who's gone?" Brynlee asked.

Boone didn't answer. He didn't *have* a good answer.

But he did need to check on Chigger again—especially if this man had gone outside.

At the thought, his employee appeared at the back door, still rubbing his head.

"I think he got away," Chigger said. "I thought I saw something run into the woods."

"Someone or something?" Boone clarified, his gaze still scanning the store for any signs of trouble.

"It was . . . it was hard to tell. At first, I thought it

was a creature. But I think it was a man, actually, wearing a coonskin hat."

"Are you okay?" Brynlee stepped toward him, examining his head with a womanly concern.

"I'll have a killer headache. But I should be fine. I could use a nurse to watch out for me, though." Chigger's eyes twinkled as he looked at Brynlee with a childlike gaze.

For some people those words would sound creepy. Coming from Chigger, they sounded humorous and playful.

But still.

"Chigger . . ." Boone warned.

He raised his hands and took a step back. "Just putting it out there."

Brynlee seemed to take it in stride as she shrugged. "I just called 911. They should be here soon."

As if on cue, sirens sounded in the background.

Boone's jaw locked as he glanced beyond Chigger at the mountainside. He didn't like this. Not at all.

They'd all come out of that relatively unscathed this time. But there was no guaranteeing that would be the case next time.

～

Brynlee stood back as she watched Boone give a statement to his brother. EMTs had arrived to check out Chigger as well, and a deputy looked for any evidence around the store.

She remained near the office, trying to stay out of the way.

She still couldn't believe that had happened. Sometimes it seemed like the whole incident had been a figment of her imagination. And then reality came crashing back.

Whoever was behind these attacks was still coming for her. Having Boone by her side wouldn't change that. A chill rushed through her.

As Sheriff Wilder stepped outside to take a phone call, Boone sauntered over to her. The concern in his eyes touched her more than it should.

It was good to have someone looking out for you . . . the only problem was Brynlee had hired Boone for the job. Was that what her future would look like? Hiring people to take care of her because she didn't have anyone else? Sometimes she felt so alone that she was certain that would be her fate.

"You sure you're okay?" Boone asked.

Brynlee nodded and pushed a hair behind her ear. "Yeah, I'm fine. Just a little stunned."

"I think we all are."

"How's Chigger?" She pointed with her head toward him.

The man was outside, sitting on the edge of the ambulance. He looked fine as he joked with the EMTs who treated him. She couldn't make out what they were saying, but Chigger seemed to be making the best of the situation.

Boone followed her gaze. "He's going to have a headache, but I think he'll be okay."

"That's good news, at least." Brynlee pulled her arms over her chest, her voice shifting to the serious. "Did he get a look at this guy's face, by chance?"

Boone frowned. "No, he didn't. Apparently, everything happened too fast."

"Did I hear him say that this man wore a coon-skin hat? Was that the only part of him that looked like an animal?"

"That's my understanding. He wasn't wearing a full costume of fur, if that's what you're asking."

"So maybe this wasn't the same guy." She felt her lips curling down. But what about the scratching sound she'd heard? It was similar to the sound she'd heard outside her chalet, only more subtle. However, there hadn't been any marks outside the door today. She'd checked for herself.

"I can't imagine there would be two people coming after you. You're sure this . . . this person you saw kill the men . . . was covered in fur?"

"Positive. Like I said, I thought he was a bear at first." Brynlee studied Boone's face. "You still don't believe me, do you? You still think I saw a bear and that I'm crazy to entertain the idea that it was a person dressed like a bear."

He rubbed his jaw a moment before shrugging. "I mean, you have to admit that it sounds outlandish."

"Maybe. But that doesn't mean it's not true."

Sheriff Wilder stepped back into the store and walked toward them. "I'm going to need you two to stick around here for a while. Is that going to be a problem?"

Boone glanced at Brynlee, waiting for her response.

"I just need to make a few phone calls," she finally said. "If I could use your office to do that . . ."

"Of course."

"Great, then. I'll be out of your hair."

18

Boone felt the pressure of everything pressing against him.

First Todd. And now this. Add to that the fact that he'd promised to protect Brynlee, and that task was beginning to feel impossible.

If only two things had happened, he might be able to dismiss that as a coincidence.

But there was no way he could deny that someone was deliberately targeting Brynlee. He just couldn't understand why.

Luke finally left two hours after arriving at the store. Boone decided to shut down business for the day. He just needed time away from this place. Besides, Brynlee had hired him, and here he was making her tag along with him. She hadn't complained, and he was grateful for that.

He wandered toward the office in time to hear the end of her phone call.

"That sounds great. You're available tomorrow? Okay. Let me know what you find out. Thank you." She pulled her phone away and smiled a little too quickly at Boone. "Hey, there. You finished?"

He nodded. "Yeah, how about you?"

"Yeah, I'm good." She stood and stretched.

He walked beside her toward his truck, neither in a hurry. "So, where to now?"

She paused and frowned. "I . . . don't know. I hadn't thought that far ahead. Is there anything you need to do?"

"I was going to have a few people over to my place for wings and to play pool. Nothing important."

"Then you should do that."

He raised his brows. "Really?"

"Yeah, I'm okay with wings and pool."

"Are you sure? Because you don't really seem like the type." No, she seemed like the type who would like fancy restaurants and days at the spa.

"Then don't make assumptions. You might be surprised what I'm like when I don't feel like my life is on the line."

What was she like? These circumstances were extraordinary. They brought out the best and worst in people. He'd seen—and experienced—that many times in his life. There were do-overs he wished he could make happen. But that wasn't reality. The truth was that people had to learn to live with the best and worst in people.

He let out an airy chuckle. "I stand corrected then. Would you like some wings and pool at my place tonight?"

"That sounds like a great distraction from everything else—although I'll pass on the wings."

"Then let's go. But first, we'll pick up your SUV and drop it by your place. Sound good?"

She nodded. "It does."

For a moment, everything felt normal. But Boone knew deep down inside that this was far from being over and far from being normal.

Brynlee fixed herself a glass of ice water. She'd had fun downstairs playing pool and darts, but now she wanted a moment of quiet. She'd escaped upstairs under the guise of getting a drink.

Her cheeks heated every time she remembered just how close Boone had been to overhearing details of her phone call. She wasn't ready for him to know all the details of her visit yet. She wasn't sure he'd understand. In fact, she was pretty sure he *wouldn't* understand.

"Hey, you must be Brynlee," someone said behind her.

She turned from putting some ice in a glass and saw a pretty brunette with long curly hair standing at the breakfast bar and staring at her.

"I am," Brynlee said.

The woman extended her hand and flashed a smile. "I'm Harper, Luke's wife. Luke, the sheriff. It's nice to meet you."

"It's nice to meet you also." Brynlee wiped her hands, getting the cold bits of ice off before shaking Harper's hand. The smell of spicy wings drifted from downstairs as well as a catchy country tune. The crowd at Boone's place was fun-loving and relaxed— just the kind of people she'd expected Boone to hang out with.

She'd met Boone's best friend, Abe. Another friend named Fowler. Ansley had stopped by for a bit, her "flavor of the month," as Boone had called him, in tow. Chigger was also there.

Harper leaned on the bar, a warm smile on her face. "So, what brings you this way? I'm also an outsider. I came here to Fog Lake about six months ago under some pretty extraordinary circumstances."

"My dad always talked about how beautiful Dead Man's Bluff was. Before he died a few months ago, I made a promise to him that I'd come here, see what the fuss was all about, and spread part of his ashes there." The words rolled off her tongue so easily. . . they were true but . . . it wasn't as simple as Brynlee made it sound.

"I'm sorry for your loss, but that sounds wonderful that you're able to still connect with your father like that."

"I hope so. I feel like it will bring some closure, I suppose."

Harper turned slightly and leaned closer. "So you hired Boone?"

"I did. I'm still trying to figure out if that's a mistake or not."

Harper smiled. "I just adore Boone. He's a good guy."

"Yeah, he proved that today." The man had done everything in his power to protect her. He'd shown little fear and more skill than she'd assumed he had.

Then again, his brother had said he'd been an Army Ranger. She shouldn't be surprised.

"I heard about what happened at the shop." Harper shuddered. "I'm sorry about what you've been through since you've been here. It's not always like that in Fog Lake."

"It's been unexpected, to say the least." At the most, Brynlee knew she'd find resistance. But she never thought she'd fear for her life like this.

"Well, you're here tonight. So I say you try to

relax and have a good time. Sometimes, that can be the best medicine."

"I agree. So how about a game of pool?"

"You're on."

But before they stepped down into the basement, Boone emerged with a big smile on his face. "Guess what?"

"What?" Harper asked.

"Luke just called. Jason Sawyer was able to track the bear prints from around the scene of the crime. They caught the bear they think is responsible for killing those men. They tranquilized him and will be doing some tests. They said he's about thirty pounds underweight, which would give him a reason to attack. It looks like we might be able to rest easier."

"But Boone . . ." Brynlee hated to be a killjoy. "That wasn't a bear in your store earlier. You and I both know that."

He didn't look deterred. "No, it wasn't a bear. I think it was someone who heard your story and wanted to use that as an excuse to come into my place."

"Why would someone do that?" Boone wasn't making sense. Not to Brynlee, at least.

"There are people in this town who want my store to close. And what better way to make that happen than by staging something like that."

"Are you talking about Todd?" Harper asked.

"You know that man has it out for me."

"You think he'd take it this far?"

"I wouldn't put anything past him."

Brynlee still wasn't sure exactly what Boone was implying. But it seemed clear that he thought these were two separate incidents. There had been the murders in the woods. And then the event at his store.

Then what about the claw marks on her car? Outside her chalet door? How were they to be explained?

Brynlee wanted to smile. Wanted to be happy. She really did.

But that creature she'd seen hadn't been a bear . . . and she didn't care what anyone said.

F *inish her.*

No, there are better ways. Legal ways. Less violent ways.

But the ways of the past—those laws—are much more effective. They were less about grace and more about swift punishment. People don't forget being punished. They are less likely to do the crimes again— much like a child being beaten with a switch.

But all those people who died . . . at his hands . . . they haunted him. Their images stabbed at his thoughts when he tried to rest.

He clenched his hands. Unclenched them.

Despite the war raging inside him, his hunger remained.

Hunger for blood. For justice.

That woman should not think she could come into town and change everything about their way of life here at Fog Lake. The arrogance caused bile to rise in him.

They needed to protect this area.

He needed to protect this area.

His fingers rubbed the bark of the tree again. How he loved bark.

Most people didn't understand bark's purpose. It protected the trees from predators.

He thought of himself like a tree. He blended in. He was hardly noticed. Yet he was essential to the area, whether people ever acknowledged him or not.

And, like bark protected a tree, he protected this town.

He watched the house. Watched the chalet where she stayed.

It was dark now, but she would be returning soon.

Until then, he would wait.

The growl started inside him again. The one that sounded deep in his gut. The one no one could hear but him.

At first, at least.

But when he unleashed the beast, no one could deny it.

And that beast was clawing to get out. Clawing

for escape. Clawing to eliminate the ones who'd invaded his land.

Soon, he told himself. *Soon*.

20

Boone was smiling still as he led Brynlee back to his truck. All his friends had left, and the night had been fun. It had been good to unwind and forget about his problems for a moment.

The most surprising thing tonight had been Brynlee. Though she'd seemed so scared since they'd met, this evening he'd seen a different side of her. She smiled, laughed, had fun.

And she was a really good pool player. She'd even beaten him once.

There was something about her that made it hard for Boone to take his eyes off her. It wasn't that he was attracted to her—nor was it that he *wasn't* attracted to her. However, that wasn't what this was about. Brynlee just had a way about her that made him curious.

There was more to Brynlee than she let on. Boone wanted to know what that was.

Then again, he had some secrets of his own. Maybe some things were best left as a mystery.

"Thanks for including me tonight," Brynlee said, once they climbed in his truck.

"Thanks for being a good sport and tagging along with me today." She'd been surprisingly pleasant company.

"I know the arrangement has been unusual and unplanned."

His mind wandered to how this evening had played out. He was left with only one question. "How'd you get so good at pool? You don't strike me as the type."

Brynlee shrugged, like it wasn't a big deal. "My mom spent a lot of time on the road, playing and singing at some seedy places. When she was doing warmups, I would play pool, trying to pass time to entertain myself."

Boone let out a grunt. That wasn't what he'd expected her to say. "Really? I guess you can never make assumptions. I would have never guessed that."

"You thought I grew up rich?" Brynlee stared at him, as if watching his reaction.

He shrugged before apologetically saying, "You do have that vibe."

"I worked for my money. Like I said, my mom tried to make it on the music scene. I grew up following her from venue to venue. Usually they were small. Bars. Coffee houses. Little festivals."

A new picture of Brynlee began to form in his mind. "Did she ever make it big time?"

"No, but she never stopped trying. In fact, she died four years ago in a car accident while on the road traveling."

Hearing that only confirmed to Boone that Brynlee was navigating life alone. The thought gripped him in ways it shouldn't. "I'm sorry to hear that."

"Yeah, me too."

Boone's thoughts continued to wander as they headed down the road. "And you also lost your father?"

"I did. But . . . well, it's a long story. I didn't actually know him until about a year ago. My mom kept me from him. He actually did a DNA test, and that's how he found me."

Her life sounded like it needed its own TV movie. "Sounds like a fascinating story."

A sad smile stretched across her lips. "Maybe I'll tell you more sometime."

"I'd like that." And he would. He wanted to know

more about this woman. About how she got to the point where she was today.

It only took a few minutes to reach her chalet. Though Luke had said they'd captured the supposed bear behind the attacks, Boone still surveyed the area around them as he escorted Brynlee inside. Until Boone knew something for sure, he'd be on guard.

Inside, Boone checked the house. It was clear.

Brynlee turned toward him. "Look, I know it's late, but I'm wired, for some reason. Would you like some tea? I've got some fruity flavors without caffeine."

He wasn't much of a tea person. "I think I'm good."

She frowned and started to say something.

"—but I'll sit with you if you'd like some," he finished.

She closed her mouth and smiled. "Okay. Thanks. I'd like the company. Do you think we could sit on the balcony upstairs? It's enclosed, so we should be safe. And it would be nice to get some fresh air."

"That sounds nice."

A few minutes later, they had blankets. Brynlee had a mug of tea. And they sat on some chunky chairs, watching the moon as it hung over Fog Lake.

True to form, the fog blanketed the water, giving everything an eerie feel.

Boone sucked in a deep breath of fresh air, enjoying the moment. This was his kind of relaxation. The only way nature was better enjoyed was when he camped in the woods and sat around a bonfire chatting with his friends. He'd always believed the simple things in life brought the most pleasure.

Brynlee shifted toward him, that twinkle back in her eyes. "So, you actually did protect me earlier."

"What kind of man do you think I am?" He offered mock offense, a hand going over his heart.

She shrugged. "I guess I wasn't sure. I had some doubts."

His smile slipped. "I'm sorry if I gave you a hard time."

"No, it's okay. It really is. I just . . . well, I've been on my own for so long that I'm not used to depending on other people."

"Is that why you started up that trail by yourself?"

"Maybe . . . I mean, I thought my boyfriend was going to come with me." She frowned, looking embarrassed for bringing it up.

His eyes widened at her revelation. "Your boyfriend?"

"He's an ex-boyfriend since I caught him with my best friend."

"Ouch."

"Yeah, ouch."

"That really stinks."

"Tell me about it."

A few minutes of silence passed. And then Boone cleared his throat. A thought had weighed heavy on his mind. He knew he didn't owe Brynlee anything. But he wouldn't be able to sleep unless he shared something with her.

"Listen, Brynlee, here's something you should know," he started, already regretting this conversation. But what kind of man would he be if he didn't tell her?

She turned toward him, curiosity glistening in her eyes. "What's that?"

He swallowed hard before blurting, "I'm responsible for Katherine's death, just like Nancy told you."

Brynlee felt everything go still around her. "What are you talking about?"

"Katherine was my wife," Boone finally said. The features of his face seemed to pull downward with grief and sadness.

Brynlee's breath caught. *Was* his wife. What did

that mean? Was Katherine the woman in the picture in his office?

"Your wife?" Brynlee's voice came out scratchy. "I'm sorry to hear that. But . . . I don't understand."

"Katherine and I started to date in high school. She was the love of my life. But her family made me promise she would go to college and get a degree before we got married. I honored that. Meanwhile, I joined the army. Made it to special forces even."

"That's a huge accomplishment."

"As soon as Katherine graduated, I proposed. I'd fulfilled my promise to her parents."

"It's good that you kept your word."

The muscles at his neck looked strained as he continued. "Her family never really liked me."

"I find that hard to believe." Brynlee's voice teetered between sincerity and teasing.

Boone raised an eyebrow. "But do you?"

"No, I really do. I mean, you can be infuriating. Totally and completely infuriating, for that matter. But you also have a way with people."

"Thanks . . . I think. But Katherine's family is one of the more affluent families here in town. My dad was the sheriff and . . . well, being the sheriff, sometimes you make enemies."

"I can imagine."

"Despite that, Katherine and I were in love. She'd taken a job here as a physical trainer and had opened a gym. She loved anything to do with exercise and adventure."

"Sounds like you were perfect together."

"Yeah, I thought so." His voice dipped again with sadness. "We got married six months later in a simple ceremony."

Brynlee held her breath, sensing there was a big change coming to his story.

"For our honeymoon, all she wanted to do was hike up to Dead Man's Bluff. It was her absolute favorite hike. The views up there . . . I mean, they're amazing. If you ask me, they rival Clingman's Dome."

Brynlee's heart stuttered in her chest as more pieces began to click in place.

"When we got close to the top, Kat decided she wanted to race. She was going to go one way, and I was supposed to go the other, and we were going to see who got to the top first. It was just the way she was. Always competitive and always wanting to push herself." His voice trailed with wistfulness.

"You don't have to finish if you don't want to." Brynlee pulled the blanket around her, suddenly chilly.

"No, it's okay. I don't talk about this . . . well, hardly ever. But I want to finish." He swallowed hard, all his features tight. "I went to the top. And I was feeling victorious because I beat her. I wandered down the trail to see how far away she was, and I saw her." Boone's voice caught.

Brynlee laid her hand on his arm, feeling her heart fill with compassion. She wanted to tell Boone not to finish . . . but he'd already made it clear that he wanted to. Instead, she remained quiet and let him gather his thoughts.

"She was at the bottom of the cliff. Her climbing equipment had malfunctioned. Before I even got to her, I knew she was dead." His voice caught, and he stared straight ahead, looking stoic as he recounted the tragedy.

"I'm so sorry, Boone."

"When her family says it was my fault, it's true. I should have double-checked her equipment. I should have insisted that we stick together. I should have . . . done a million things differently. And I would have. If I'd known."

"I think we can all say that about certain times in our lives."

"Her family has blamed me since then. At times, they've actually accused me of doing something to her purposefully. They even took me to court in a civil case."

"Why would they do that?"

"They needed someone to blame, and grief can do strange things to people."

"I can't argue that."

Brynlee's half-brothers had certainly been abrasive after her dad had died. They'd done everything they could to let Brynlee know she wasn't a part of their family. Brynlee was used to being alone, though. As much as she might like the idea of having brothers, it wasn't worth it to fight for a relationship with them.

But there had to be more to Boone's story. "Why would her family accuse you of that, though? I mean, what could they possibly think your motive was?"

"Quite simply? Money. That's what they ascertained, at least. The truth is, money has never been all that important to me. I just want enough to live on."

Brynlee studied him a moment. "You need money right now for your store, don't you?"

"I'm not going to kill someone to get it, if that's what you're asking."

"I wasn't trying to imply that in the least."

He frowned again and rubbed his chin. "There was a mudslide not far from here about two months ago. A few boulders fell into the creek about a hundred yards from my store. The county caught wind of it, and now they say I need to pay to secure the rocks on the mountainside near Falling Timbers. They say it's a safety hazard and they can condemn my store if I don't comply."

"Yikes. Won't insurance cover it?"

"Nope. Because nothing has happened. This is all precautionary. Personally, I think the county wants to see me shut down. The inspector has never liked me, and he's using this as an excuse to make my life miserable."

"Man, that stinks." So, that was what the ordeal had been about. "Do you mind if I ask how much something like that would cost?"

"Upwards of twenty thousand."

"Can you get a loan?"

"Maybe. But the problem is that Katherine's family owns all the banks in the area."

"Ouch." That could be a problem, couldn't it?

"Yeah, ouch." Boone's gaze froze on something below them, and he stood. His muscles seemed to tighten in the blink of an eye. "Brynlee, you need to get inside."

"What's going on?"

His voice sounded dead serious as he said, "Someone is in the woods."

Fear raced through her. Brynlee didn't argue. Instead, she darted into her bedroom and began praying.

21

Boone drew his weapon as he hurried down the stairs.

He'd yelled for Brynlee to call 911. Help should be on the way soon.

But this guy was brazen showing up here again.

Guy?

Yes, it looked like a man out there.

Boone was having trouble reconciling who was behind these acts. But he knew enough to know whatever was going on, it wasn't safe for Brynlee. And he didn't like this.

He reached the first floor, and instantly his muscles tightened.

He had no idea where this guy had gone now. Was he still lurking in the woods? What was his end game?

Peering through the window, Boone glanced outside—though just barely.

Trees stared back.

For a moment, he was transported back in time. Back to when he'd been an Army Ranger.

The difference was, back then, he'd known who his enemy was. Right now, he had no idea who this faceless thing was.

Despite that, he still felt like he was in a war zone and he was waiting for the moment of attack.

Boone stayed still. Painfully still.

He didn't want to give away his location. No, he needed the upper hand right now.

As the minutes ticked past, he decided to peer out again. He wanted to see if this guy was still there. If he had gotten closer.

He just had to move quickly and quietly.

Just as Boone leaned toward the window, glass shattered.

Boone jumped back as he saw something fly through the air.

His gaze went to the wall across from him.

An axe had imbedded itself there.

That man had thrown an axe into the house, wedging it perfectly into the wall. That could have easily been his skull.

Boone hoped the police would get here—and fast.

Brynlee pressed herself against the wall of her dark bedroom. Glass broke downstairs, shattering the silence. She sucked back a scream.

What was going on down there? Was Boone okay?

That had definitely been glass breaking. Maybe a window.

Was the man inside her house?

Panic surged through her.

Sure, the cops may have captured that bear . . . but a bear wasn't behind these crimes.

A man was.

And that man was at her chalet right now.

Brynlee prayed the cops got here soon.

How could she just stay up here when Boone might be in trouble? It seemed like such a cowardly thing to do. What if he was hurt?

Before she could question herself, she darted toward the window and ducked below it. Maybe Brynlee could see what was going on outside.

The lights were off upstairs. Maybe whoever was out there wouldn't see her.

On the count of three, she raised herself up from the floor. Her face slowly rose until her eyes caught sight of the world outside.

As she did, movement caught her eye.

It was the man.

Standing just below her window.

Staring up at her.

She started to duck again. But, before she could, the man jerked his arm.

The next instant, Brynlee saw something hurtle through the air.

Brynlee sucked in a breath and dove out of the way as something crashed through the window.

She glanced at the floor beside her and let out a scream. In the midst of the broken glass lay an axe.

An axe?

What was going on here?

22

Boone froze as he heard more glass breaking. A thump. A scream.

He darted upstairs.

Had the man somehow gotten to Brynlee? No, there was no way. No outdoors stairs led to the second level.

Unless the man had somehow scaled the house . . . which was unlikely. But Boone didn't want to rule anything out either.

Come on, Luke. Where are you? Some backup would be nice right now.

Boone stopped at the top of the steps and glanced at the carnage there.

Another axe lay on the floor, making it look like a massacre had occurred here. Broken glass from the window surrounded it, some shards large and knife-like and others only beads.

Brynlee was sprawled on the floor only feet away, terror on her face. She sat up, stray pieces of glass falling from her hair.

Adrenaline pounded through him as he rushed toward her. "Are you okay?"

She nodded, her expression still as frail as her voice sounded. "I'm fine."

His jaw flexed as determination seized his muscles. He glanced out the broken window in time to see the dark figure run into the woods. A new determination solidified inside him.

"I'm going to go get this guy," he muttered, starting toward the door.

"Be careful." Brynlee's wide eyes met his, and worry captured her voice.

"I will be."

Boone charged down the stairs, desperate not to lose this psycho. He had his gun, and their lives had most definitely been threatened. This needed to end before someone else got hurt—or worse.

As he ran outside, he spotted the police lights flashing nearby. Luke joined him mid-stride as he jogged toward the woods.

"He went this way," Boone said, gripping his gun. "I just saw him."

"Let's get this guy." Luke's voice sounded hard with determination.

Deputy Cruise ran beside them, his breaths coming fast and heavy.

The man couldn't have gotten too far away. He'd just been right here. Outside the house.

The three of them raced into dark woods. The thick foliage instantly surrounded them, but a small path had been cut leading down to the lake. Had the man gone down this way?

It was a good starting place.

They continued to charge forward, deeper into the woods. But an air of caution grew around them. They needed to be on guard. Luke shone his flashlight ahead of them.

As he did, the beam illuminated something in the distance.

A figure stood in front of them.

Boone stopped, as did Luke and Deputy Cruise.

The three of them stared at the man standing on the path facing them.

It was Big Ben.

He stared at them blankly, not moving. He held nothing in his hands. But it was almost like he'd been waiting for them to arrive.

But why? What sense did all of this make?

Boone braced himself for a battle. He waited for the unknown. For enemy tactics.

"Big Ben, what are you doing here?" Luke asked, gripping his gun with one hand and a flashlight with the other.

The man stared back but remained silent, expressionless. An axe was wedged beneath his belt.

"We're going to need to take you into the station," Luke continued, his voice even but authoritative. "Put your hands in the air."

Big Ben did as they asked. Deputy Cruise cuffed him and escorted him without issue to the squad car.

That had been much easier than Boone had anticipated. He bit back a frown, something not feeling right in his gut. Why would Big Ben give himself up like that? For that matter, why would he do any of this?

"I'm going to go check on Brynlee," Boone said, desperate to make sure this wasn't another distraction.

"Careful not to disturb any of the evidence inside," Luke called.

"I won't. But we're going to need to find somewhere else to stay tonight." No way would either of them feel safe staying in this chalet after what happened, not to mention the windows had been broken.

"I'll call Harper."

Boone paused for long enough to give his brother a hard, inquisitive look. "Really?"

Boone assumed that Luke would want to keep his wife as far away from this as he could. His brother wasn't a doter, but he adored his new bride and left no doubt that he was crazy about her.

"Really," Luke said. "I'll see if you two can stay with us, at least for tonight. After that, I make no promises. But Harper, if anyone, understands what it's like to be in this kind of danger."

That was right. Harper had almost died.

Boone's throat clenched. Brynlee's life was also in danger.

He couldn't let someone else die on his watch. He knew that for certain. He would do everything in his power to stop any more harm from coming to Brynlee—whether he was being paid or not.

Three hours later, Boone and Brynlee had packed their bags and gone to Luke and Harper's place. Brynlee was grateful to have a safe place to go, but she hated to impose on the sheriff and his wife. The two lived in a little three-bedroom cottage that had access to the lake below.

After they'd each been shown their separate rooms, Harper had offered them some cookies and tea, which sounded nice. Besides, Brynlee needed to unwind. No way would she be able to sleep with so much on her mind.

As they sat in a cozy living room nibbling on the treats, they chitchatted with Harper. Brynlee already liked the woman—and she noted that Harper had excellent decorating taste.

But Brynlee was just biding her time. She was ready to hear an update. She was wired, unable to sleep and wouldn't until she knew what the sheriff had found out.

Finally, just past three a.m., she heard a truck pull up to the cottage. They all seemed to hear it and stiffened with anticipation.

Luke had returned to the house.

As the front door opened, Boone stood to greet him. He wasted no time in asking his brother, "Well?"

Luke paused by the entryway to the living room and leaned against the doorframe. "Big Ben hasn't said a word. He has the capability to speak, but he doesn't. This time is no different."

Brynlee's heart sank at his pronouncement. She'd been hoping for something solid. For answers. For an end to this nightmare. "You'd think he'd want to defend himself if he was innocent."

"You'd think. But we were able to search his house." Luke moved into the room and perched on the edge of a leather recliner near where Harper sat. "We found evidence that he's been feeding the bears around his house."

"What?" Brynlee asked. Did people do that?

Luke nodded solemnly. "It's true. There are all kinds of bear prints in the ground near his back door. There was bear fur in his house—not like a bear skin rug. But evidence that he may be letting the creatures into his house."

"Why would he do that?" Boone asked, looking just as perplexed.

"Maybe he's not quite right in the head," Harper offered. "I read a newspaper article once about a woman who lived in the woods and fed the bears every day. She began to think of them as family. Unfortunately, one day her body was found in the woods. She'd been mauled to death. Wild animals are just that—wild and unpredictable."

Brynlee shivered at the thought of it.

"Do you think Big Ben has been training the bears?" Boone asked.

"I'd say it was a possibility," Luke said. "It's too early to say anything for sure, but it looks like he could be our guy."

"Why would Big Ben be behind this?" Boone leaned back and ran a hand over his hair. "What could possibly be his motive?"

"He's always been strange," Luke said. "Everyone

in town knows that. You know he's always wandering these woods and that he feels some kind of connection with the mountains. You remember that time he chased off some hikers who started a fire during a burn ban?"

"I know he scared them enough that they filed charges against him," Boone said. "But Big Ben didn't harm them. They shouldn't have started that fire, and Big Ben should have used a better method. Besides, there's a difference between being eccentric and being a cold-blooded killer."

Luke let out a long breath, looking exhausted. "I'm not arguing that. But all the evidence right now is pointing to him. You saw him outside the house tonight yourself. He had an axe. It looks like he's the one who threw two axes into Brynlee's cabin. He could have killed you both."

"Yes." Boone frowned and leaned forward as an unseen weight seemed to press on him. "But this just doesn't make sense."

"Crazy doesn't make sense," Luke said. "You and I both know that."

"Yes, we do," Boone muttered.

Luke grabbed his hat, placed it on his head, and then picked up his keys. "I just wanted to stop by and give you the update. I figured you'd all be waiting up, anxious to know what was going on."

Brynlee was grateful that he'd been courteous

enough to do that, though she'd wished for something more definite. Still, she said, "We appreciate it."

Luke turned to Harper, who sat on an ottoman next to him. "I have to get back to the station."

"I figured you would." She reached up and gave her husband a quick kiss. "Take care of yourself. You look tired."

At the sight of the tenderness between them, Brynlee's heart lurched.

That was what she wanted in her own life. But there were times she knew with certainty that she would never find it.

Based on her time here so far, she might not survive to see that happen.

23

Brynlee's thoughts still churned the next morning.

She'd slept surprisingly well. The bed was comfortable and warm. She felt safe knowing Boone was just in the next room.

But, right now, she lay in bed trying to contend with her feelings before she got up and faced everyone. She replayed what had happened yesterday as well as the conversation with Luke in the middle of the night.

Like Boone, she wasn't convinced that Big Ben was behind all this either. But at least someone had been arrested. Big Ben had definitely been dangerous. He'd most likely thrown those axes into the chalet.

She agreed with Boone, though. Why would he do this? Was it just because he was crazy?

However, the bears made him look guilty, as did the fact Big Ben had been caught in the woods near the chalet. The additional fact that he didn't talk obviously made it difficult for them to get answers.

But what if this too-good-to-believe turn of events was actually true? What if Big Ben was behind all these crimes, and now he was behind bars?

That would free Brynlee to do what she'd come here to Fog Lake to do.

Hope surged inside her.

Maybe her efforts hadn't been wasted.

She needed to climb up Dead Man's Bluff. But she knew she couldn't do it alone. Not after what had happened last time.

She had to see if Boone would come with her.

She sat up in bed and grabbed her bag from the floor beside her. She pulled a piece of paper from it.

It was a torn page from her father's old journal. He'd given it to her. On it, there were a few scribbled notes and a hand-drawn map of the area around Dead Man's Bluff.

There was a cabin on the map.

A cabin that she needed to get inside. Apparently, a deed had been left there. She'd need it in order for some of those permits to go through. That's what her attorney had told her, at least.

Without wasting any more time, Brynlee climbed out of bed, hurried across the hall, showered, and dressed. She glanced at her reflection in the mirror as she pulled on an evergreen-colored sweatshirt.

Her mom had taught her the importance of making a good first impression. They might not have had money for food, but her mom had always looked nice. Brynlee let out a cynical laugh.

Though she'd tried not to emulate her mom in that regard, Brynlee's job as an interior designer also required her to look nice. However, when Brynlee wasn't working, she was perfectly happy to wear yoga pants and baggy T-shirts. Image really wasn't as important to her as people might think.

By the time she got downstairs, Boone and Harper were exchanging playful jabs at each other at the breakfast table. Playful jabs were apparently what Boone did best.

She paused for a minute and observed Boone. He was freshly showered also, with wet hair. He wore his customary jeans and T-shirt with a flannel shirt over it, unbuttoned.

Her throat felt unreasonably dry as she realized just how handsome the man was. Too handsome for his own good. Handsome enough that she should stay away.

"Good morning," Harper called when she spotted Brynlee. "Have a seat, and I'll get you some breakfast. Boone told me you're a vegetarian. I just so happened to have made a tasty fruit salad, and I have some organic bread and fresh peanut butter."

"That sounds wonderful. Thank you." She lowered herself beside Boone and offered a smile that almost felt shy.

Shy? Why in the world would she feel shy around Boone?

Or maybe it wasn't Boone that had caused the reaction. Maybe it was the situation. Maybe it was the fact that this breakfast almost felt like more than Boone just doing his job—it felt like she'd been taken into his family.

Her cheeks flushed at the absurd thought. This was clearly a professional arrangement, and that was all.

The fruit salad and peanut butter toast were tasty. And Brynlee enjoyed the lighthearted conversation between Boone and his sister-in-law. She learned that Harper worked doing marketing for the town. That at one time she'd been a journalist.

When they finished eating, Boone turned toward her, his arms crossed against his muscular chest and an amused expression on his face. "So, what today, Boss?"

Brynlee licked her lips, unsure how to even ask what she needed to ask him.

"You're still on the clock then?" she started.

"Until you fire me."

She decided to launch into her request and be direct instead of beating around the bush. "Great. Because I need you to take me to Dead Man's Bluff."

Boone blinked, certain he hadn't heard Brynlee correctly. "Come again?"

She shrugged as if her request had been as simple as asking him to make a pot of coffee. "No one knows the mountain better than you. I need to make it to the top."

He shook his head, his head dipping toward the table at the absurdity of her statement. "No, I think that's a terrible idea."

Behind him, Boone saw Harper slip out of the way. No doubt, she sensed the conversation would get heated. She knew him well enough to know that.

"I need to go up there," Brynlee continued. "It's the whole reason I came into town."

Boone raised his hands with frustration. "There's

a killer out there. What's so important that you would want to go up there still?"

Brynlee raised her chin. "Sheriff Wilder thinks he has that man in custody."

"You don't even believe that. You said so yourself last night. I mean, I'm all for being optimistic but . . . there's a fine line between optimistic and stupid."

"I am a skeptic, and I know this arrest seems too good to be true. But . . ."

"And what if it is too good to be true?" Boone stared at her, watching her reaction.

Brynlee shrugged and looked off into the distance, as if trying to find the right words. "The bear they think was behind the attacks is in custody and so is the man who was throwing axes at us while we were in the house. Between the two of them, I think we should feel more confident that the danger has been extinguished."

He let out a quick laugh and ran a hand over his face. He didn't want to be disrespectful but . . . Brynlee had no idea how dangerous that mountain was, even when a killer wasn't on the loose. "I doubt that."

She drew in a long breath and nodded as if her mind was made up. "Okay. I knew this might be your reaction, and that's fine. You don't have to take me up there. I don't want you to do anything you're not comfortable with."

She didn't sound offended, only determined.

Oh, no. Boone knew exactly what she was doing. "You're going to go up there without me, aren't you?"

"I'm going up that mountain, yes. It's why I came here. I don't have all the time in the world. I have clients I have appointments with next week. My life is waiting for me back in Pennsylvania."

That's right. Brynlee would leave here soon. She wasn't a permanent fixture around here. Boone would be wise to remember that—to remember not to get too close to someone who wasn't sticking around.

"It's like a death wish," he finally said.

"I don't know what to say." She shrugged again. "I can do the trip in a day. It might not be easy, but it's doable."

More irritation climbed up his spine. "And if you get hurt?"

"I call for help."

"Cell phone service is spotty."

Her determined gaze didn't waver. "Then I'll wait for another hiker."

"No one wants to hike that area right now—no one but you." Brynlee was being way too naïve about this.

"Then I'll figure something out." She stared back at him, equally as stubborn as he was.

Boone raked a hand through his hair. She was serious. Dead serious. "I'm just speechless."

"Actually, you're not. You keep talking." Brynlee took a step back and gave him a pointed look. "Now, if you don't mind, I need to start preparing."

He grabbed her arm before she got too far away. He had to talk some sense into her. "This is a terrible idea, Brynlee."

"Life is full of terrible ideas."

This woman . . . she was impossible. Stubborn. Determined. And she ignited something in him that no one had touched in years. Boone wasn't sure how he felt about that.

As he stared at her and wrestled with thoughts, he felt his muscles bristle. He was just as determined and stubborn as any Wilder might be, but he also couldn't ignore his protective side.

"Fine," he finally said. "I'll go."

He already regretted the words, and they'd just left his lips.

Brynlee observed him a moment. He couldn't read her expression. She didn't exactly look satisfied but maybe relieved.

"No pressure," she told him. "I don't want you to do anything you're not comfortable with."

He let out a skeptical grunt. "But we're not going today."

"Why not?"

"Several reasons. The weather is iffy today. Plus, we should have already started, and it will take at least two or three hours to properly pack for the trip. We don't want to hike in the dark. We should go tomorrow and use today to prepare." And to wait for any updates, he thought to himself.

Brynlee observed him a moment before nodding. "Okay, it's a deal."

At least he'd won that battle.

24

B rynlee glanced out the window as she rode down the street in Boone's truck. Her thoughts swirled with everything that was going on.

Doing the hike tomorrow might be a better idea all around. Brynlee still had people to talk to and some business to attend to. She couldn't forget about those things. Her reason for coming here was anything but simple. Promises rarely were.

But it would be harder and harder to keep her secret as she filed more permits and did more research. And Brynlee knew now with even more clarity that her ideas probably wouldn't be welcome here. These people who had let her into their lives— people like Boone, Luke, and Harper—were sure to be disappointed in her. Maybe even feel betrayed.

Yet, if she didn't do this, she'd be going against her father's wishes.

Pressure built inside her at the thought. Maybe she should tell Boone the whole truth.

She just had to wait for the right opportunity. Her nerves built up inside her until she felt shaky.

Why was she being such a wimp?

She knew why.

Because when she told him, it would change everything.

As they pulled into downtown Fog Lake, Brynlee's eyes widened. A scurry of activity flourished in town as people set up tents and tables along Main Street. A banner had strung above the town square. She'd even seen some selfie stations on street corners—wooden cutouts where people could place their faces and make it look like they were in the mountains.

"What's going on here?" Brynlee asked.

"It's something Harper had a hand in starting called First Fridays. On the first Friday of every month, people come from all over the county and set up food trucks. We have live music in the town square. Games for the kids. Vendors sell their crafts. It's just a good way to make this town more of a community."

"That sounds great," Brynlee said realizing yet again just how perfect this little town was. Maybe it shouldn't be touched or changed. "People really love this community, don't they?"

"They do. None of the locals want this to turn into another tourist trap. I mean, we love our visitors, don't get me wrong. But we're against over-development. We don't want big box stores or chain restaurants or fancy resorts. Part of this town's charm is found in its smallness."

Brynlee swallowed hard as she processed his words. "That makes sense. But more development would mean more people and, by default, more income, right? More jobs. More security."

"Life isn't always about bringing in more income. There's a lot to be said for being content with what you have."

Maybe this was when Brynlee should tell him. Should convince him that not all change was bad. She swallowed hard before saying, "Don't get me wrong. I think this town has a lot of charm. It's just that . . . sometimes, if we're afraid of change, then we'll eventually start to die. Life is about adapting."

"I don't believe that's true here. I think people crave the simplicity of places like Fog Lake. I don't think that will ever die." Boone put his truck in Park. "And that's even more reason we can't let Dead Man's Bluff be developed."

Her throat tightened, and the words she wanted

to say died in her throat. Instead, she said, "You feel really adamant about that, don't you?"

"I do. I plan on doing everything I can to stop it from happening."

His words hung in the air.

There was no way she could tell him now.

He let out a breath and glanced at her, his shoulders softening. "Anyway, before we get sidetracked, I want to talk to Luke down at the station, and I've got to pick up some gear from Abe. We need to do those things before our hike. Sound okay?"

"Do you mind if I go with you to talk to Luke? I'd like to hear any updates also."

"We're doing this on your dime, so it's your call."

"Let's go then." But a new round of nerves fluttered inside her.

There was so much riding on Brynlee being here. She was either going to let down her father or let down Boone.

Both options made her heart squeeze with regret.

Boone paused as soon as he stepped into the Fog Lake Sheriff's Office. Voices in the background drifted out into the lobby. Was that Lonny? It sure sounded like it.

Maybe the man had some updates.

With Brynlee beside him, Boone walked toward Luke's office and paused in the doorway.

"Unfortunately, it's inconclusive," Lonny said, pointing to a paper on Luke's desk. "As much as I would like to match these claw prints, there are too many variables that make it impossible."

"I thought claw marks were like fingerprints," Luke said. "That each is unique."

"Unfortunately, it's not that simple," Lonny said. "There are a lot of variables when it comes to claw marks. And claw marks on flesh? It's very difficult to ascertain everything we need from that. We're mostly testing DNA, but it will take a few days to get back."

"And if the DNA of this bear matches that at the crime scene?" Luke asked.

"Then the bear will have to be euthanized."

Luke crossed his arms, listening intently to what Lonny said. "But what are the chances that there are two different bears behind this?"

Lonny released a breath and rubbed his chin. As he did, Boone noticed the cut on his forearm. It looked deep and long. His shirt had concealed it, but his sleeve had crept up.

As quickly as it happened, Lonny lowered his arm and tugged his sleeve down.

He didn't want anyone to see it. Interesting, Boone thought.

"I agree that the chances aren't likely that there are two different bears here," Lonny said. "However, male bears will generally only wander about fifteen miles from their habitat. The chance that a bear left the Dead Man's Bluff area and traveled down to Fog Lake, tracking someone? I've never heard of anything like that happening. It's highly unlikely, especially considering it was probably twenty miles, at least."

"What do you think about Big Ben?" Luke asked, obviously not bothered by Boone and Brynlee's presence. "About the evidence we found at his place?"

Lonny released a long breath, obviously taking this conversation very seriously. "I do think it's possible to train bears. I've seen it happen before. If a bear starts to depend on a human to feed it, then . . . it's amazing what creatures will do for food. Of course, Big Ben isn't talking. He's the only one who really knows the truth. There were no cages at his house, correct? No signs that he was keeping any animals in captivity?"

"No, no cages," Luke said. "But it did look like he's let the animals into his house. There was hair on his couch and carpet. No sign of violence, however."

Boone stepped more fully into the room, interested in seeing how Lonny reacted to his next statement. "I know how this all looks—I mean, I was there last night. I felt that axe whiz by me. A few inches to the right, and I might not be standing here right now. But I've never thought of Big Ben as being a violent man. He just likes to keep to himself. Why do this now?"

"Fact is, you never know who people are behind closed doors," Luke said. "You and I both know that."

Images of Luke's last major case flooded Boone's mind. A serial killer had haunted this area, and the man had taken everyone by surprise. Luke was right. Sometimes, the bad guy masqueraded as the person you least expected.

"There was bark stripped from some of the trees around his house," Luke continued. "Does that mean anything?"

"Doesn't Big Ben make crafts using wood?" Lonny asked. "Baskets, I believe."

"That could explain it," Luke conceded.

"The idea of a man and a wild animal being responsible does make sense," Boone added, inserting himself into the conversation again, whether or not his opinion was welcome. "I mean, maybe it was a wild animal that killed those men—one that had been manipulated by a human."

Luke sighed and leaned back. "Apparently,

people have been canceling reservations here in town."

"What?" Boone asked.

"That's what I heard this morning. Word of what happened has spread, and hikers don't want to venture out into these woods until they know they're safe. Plus, the park service is talking about closing the trails until we know something for sure. We just can't take the risk. I'm inclined to agree with them."

"But you have the bear in custody," Boone said. "I'm not convinced that the bear was behind the first incident at Brynlee's place, but I do think there's evidence a wild animal has played a part in this. How long will it take to confirm the animal was behind the attacks?"

"Longer than you'd think," Lonny said. "Obviously, if we did an autopsy on the creature, we'd know sooner. But we don't want to harm the bear. So we have to wait for the bear to empty the contents of his stomach."

Boone held back a frown. Nothing was ever fast when it came to these investigations, was it?

25

Brynlee chewed on everything she'd just heard from Lonny. Basically, it all meant that they still didn't have any answers. That didn't come as a surprise.

But she had hoped for more clarity. If she was going to take this hike, it would be nice to know the danger was mostly behind them. But maybe the danger wouldn't leave her—not while she was here in Fog Lake.

She resisted a sigh as she watched Lonny depart, leaving just the three of them in the office.

Boone lowered himself into a chair across from his brother. "What about Todd?"

"What about him?" Luke raised his brow and stared back at his brother.

"Did you find out if he was behind the incident

at the store yesterday?" Boone tapped his foot, nearly looking impatient.

"You don't think Big Ben is behind it?" Luke asked, studying his brother's face without apology.

"No, I think my store was the target of that incident—that it was separate from the rest of this. I mean, the methods don't fit, do they? There were no claw marks left on my walls or doors. No one heard any roars. No, it was nothing except a scare tactic."

"I just don't think Todd would do something like that. I know he doesn't like you, but I don't think he has it in him to knock Chigger out and try something like that." Luke shrugged as if he wished his opinion was different.

"He's the only person who makes sense, though." Boone's voice hardened. "For that matter, maybe he's working with Nancy and her family . . ."

Luke's expression softened with compassion. "I know they don't like you. I know they'd love nothing more than to see you ruined. But they're more likely to use legal means to do so, don't you think?"

Brynlee watched Boone's reaction closely, trying to get a read on the situation. It was obviously multi-layered and complex. The toll it had taken on Boone was clearly hard. Devastating, for that matter.

His jaw flexed, and he looked way. "I don't know. All I know is that I don't like what's going on here in this town."

"Just be patient," Luke said. "We'll find answers, all in good time."

Boone nodded and stood with a sigh. "Let me know if you hear anything else."

They walked outside into the temperate day, strolling down the sidewalk. To anyone watching, they might look as if they didn't have a care in the world. The sun warmed their shoulders, though the breeze was still chilly. In the background, the muted sounds of a band warming up filled the air and the smell of fried dough—funnel cakes maybe—wafted with the wind.

Brynlee's thoughts churned as she processed everything she'd just learned while talking to Luke. Not just those facts, she supposed. She was thinking about everything that had happened in the past twenty-four hours.

"You said your dad was sheriff before Luke, didn't you?" she asked, shoving her hands into the pockets of her jacket.

"That's right. He loved his job."

She hesitated just a moment before continuing. "So was he in charge of the investigation when . . ."

Boone frowned and slowed his steps. "When Katherine died? He was. He had to remain objective and keep things on the up and up or he knew the Tennessee Bureau of Investigation would take over. It was . . . uncomfortable, to say the least."

"It was all based on hearsay, though, right? I mean, there was no proof as to what went wrong. The only person who knew what really happened was your wife."

Boone paused there on the corner. The past seemed to consume his expression as he frowned and disappeared into another time. "Yes but . . . to be upfront, Kat and I took out life insurance policies on each other before we got married."

"Okay . . ." Brynlee waited for him to explain because she knew he had more to say.

"It wasn't my idea, but Kat insisted on it. Her family came from money, so she had a sizable nest egg, thanks to a trust fund set up for her."

"And, once she died, you were able to get that money . . ." Details clicked into place in her mind.

"I didn't want it. Like I said, I don't care about money."

She tugged her toboggan cap down lower as the breeze whispered down the street. "What happened to it then?"

"I gave it back to her family."

She resisted the urge to place her hand on his arm, to try and offer comfort. It wasn't her place . . . but she wanted it to be.

Maybe.

"Certainly, she would understand," she said instead.

"Maybe she would. But no one else. And she's not around anymore." He frowned and let out a long breath. "Look, I'm not trying to get terse with you. But it's a sore subject."

"I understand." But Brynlee didn't. She couldn't even begin to imagine finding the love of her life, only to lose him on their honeymoon. It would be devastating.

Boone started walking back toward his truck again, but his steps seemed heavier. "I think we should get over to Abe's place. I need to rent some of his equipment for our trip tomorrow. Sound okay?"

"Sounds fine." But a bad feeling still lingered in her gut.

Brynlee supposed it didn't matter how idyllic some people's lives might seem. Beneath the surface, everyone had their problems and struggles.

Even her.

Brynlee watched as Boone leaned against the rough wooden counter of his friend's store. He looked at ease here, at home. For a moment, she watched him in his element.

She found herself wishing earlier that Boone could see her in her natural state. She knew in her everyday life she was more bubbly and happy. She loved to laugh and smile. But, coming here, she felt all out of sorts—not like herself at all.

Abe's Outfitters was a shack-like kiosk located right on the edge of town, near the lake. Boone had explained the business to her on the way there. People rented kayaks, paddleboards, and other gear. Abe also offered excursions on occasion, and, apparently, Boone helped him when he could.

The building itself was only a little bigger than a shed, and it had a window that opened during business hours. Outside, kayaks and paddleboards were lined up against a wooden rail, just begging people to use them.

Boone had said his friend made a decent living for himself here, and that this job was perfect for him. Abe apparently lived for stuff like this, and it was just one of the reasons he and Boone had bonded.

Abe's sidekick, Fowler, was also here. At the moment, he was cleaning the kayaks near the shore. If Brynlee had the chance, she wanted to talk with him.

"So, what's the word from the trail volunteers?" Boone asked, leaning into the window.

Abe shrugged as he double-checked the life vests hanging inside the shop. "They haven't seen anything. There are some people who've gone out there just for the thrill of knowing there could be a wild animal ravaging the area. Some people are just too stubborn to cancel their plans. But I fully expect the park service to issue some warnings here soon. I'm kind of surprised they haven't already."

"It won't matter." Boone absently played with a jar full of pens that stood by a stack of clipboards. "They can't shut down Dead Man's Bluff."

"Why's that?" Brynlee asked, curious as to why they couldn't.

Abe glanced over at her, as if the question surprised him. "Because that land is privately owned. No one is supposed to be on it, but the owner apparently doesn't care."

The owner . . . Brynlee pressed her lips together for a moment before asking, "How is the owner supposed to keep people off? Aren't there signs up?"

"That's basically a liability thing." Abe adjusted the last of the life vest straps and nodded as Fowler strode toward them. "The land is right on the edge of the Great Smoky Mountains National Park. Naturally, people are going to veer off the trail, especially after one of those hiking blogs picked up an article on the area several years back. It's known as one of the best views in the Appalachian Mountains. People come from all over to test out their skills."

She shrugged, trying not to show anything. "Seems like it should be illegal."

"It is, but people want the views and the challenge of it." Abe moved to the paddles and began straightening them as Fowler listened in on the conversation. "You're going to find out soon just what this hike is about."

Brynlee frowned. "I did my research."

"Research doesn't show you zilch," Boone said, still at the counter watching everything with that simmering look in his eyes. "When you're on that trail, and you're looking at a two hundred-foot drop-off on either side of you as you hike the ridge, you'll see how dangerous it is. I hope you don't mind heights."

Truth was, Brynlee had never loved heights. Not at all.

"I like challenges," she said instead.

Boone grunted. "Well, you're going to have a big one ahead of you."

"Are you talking about the fact that I'm working with you?"

Abe and Fowler laughed and bemoaned how Brynlee was right.

Boone just gave her a look. "You'll see. I promise you that. You'll see."

26

As Boone and Abe began working on gathering the rappelling gear, Brynlee walked over to Fowler. He stood behind the building sorting through various ropes and coiling them. She remembered hearing Ansley say that Fowler was an unofficial Skookum expert.

She wanted to know what he'd seen and why he believed this creature really existed. She wasn't sure why she was so curious, but the questions pressed on her.

The man was in his early thirties, and he had dark hair, skin that had been tanned from hours of being outside, a thick beard, and a stocky build. He seemed unassuming and like a true, unapologetic mountain man. He spoke with a slow drawl and had a toothpick dangling from his mouth.

Brynlee paused beside him, checking to see if Boone and Abe were still occupied in their conversation. They were. "So, I hear you know a thing or two about Skookum."

He paused from wrapping the ropes and observed her for a moment before continuing to work. "That's right. No one believes me, but I know what I saw."

"Can you tell me about your experiences? I'm really curious. No one believes me either when I tell them what I saw. That wasn't a bear out there. But I'm not convinced it was a man either. I just . . . I don't know."

"You promise not to laugh at me?" he said. "I don't like to talk about it anymore because all the guys rib me about it."

"Yes, I honestly want to know."

Fowler let out a long breath and paused from his work. "My family has lived in this area for decades. My dad was a coalminer for his living and a bootlegger for fun. So the stories of these mountains go back for generations. There have always been rumors of Skookum in these woods."

A trickle of both fear and curiosity dripped down her spine. "When was the first time you saw one?"

He smoothed his beard. "I actually remember riding in my dad's old truck when we were coming back to the house after dropping off a 'shipment' to a buyer in town. It was at dusk, so the sun wasn't completely gone. But it was getting dark outside. As we were headed up the side of the mountain road, this creature ran out in front of the truck. My dad had to throw on his brakes, and the truck swerved."

"What was it?" Brynlee pulled her arms more tightly around her.

"That was the question. Both my dad and I sat there in the truck for several minutes, neither of us saying anything. And then my dad only said one word. *Skookum*. That's when I knew what I'd seen."

"Did it look like a bear?" Brynlee's heart rate climbed as she listened to his story. She didn't believe in mythical creatures—normally. But this whole experience had made her question everything.

"Maybe. I mean, it was furry like a bear. And it was big like a bear—like a bear standing on his hind legs." As Fowler spoke, his hands began flying, and he illustrated each point with grand gestures. "But it didn't quite move like a bear, if that makes sense. I mean, a bear walking on two legs will kind of lumber back and forth a little more. This creature moved more gracefully than that."

Brynlee glanced at Boone and saw he was still distracted. She continued. "You said that was the first time you'd seen it. Does that mean there have been other times also?"

Fowler seemed to have warmed up quickly and to enjoy telling his stories. The ropes seemed all but forgotten. "Another time I was out on the trail. I'm one of the volunteers. Again, it was getting late. I heard something moving behind me, but I knew I was the only one out there. I froze and looked behind me. I didn't see anything. But I had that feeling, you know? You can just sense when you're being watched sometimes."

"What happened?" Brynlee practically held her breath as she waited to hear the rest of the story. Another part of her hoped she wasn't being taken for a ride.

"I would take a couple of steps, and then I would hear something again. It was like I was being followed. But I never saw anyone."

Her chest deflated. She'd hoped for something more definitive. "So how are you sure it was the Skookum?"

"I wasn't . . . until I reached a fork in the trail. I decided to head back. I started that way and, as I did, I turned and looked behind me." He illustrated by looking over his shoulder. He lowered his voice as he continued. "When I did, I saw the Skookum crossing the path. It was like he'd given up on following me."

"Did he know you saw him?"

"He looked at me. When he saw me watching, he took off in a run."

She frowned. That didn't match what she'd seen. "Doesn't sound like a predator."

"I think the Skookum are only predators when they feel threatened. And I think one of them killed my father. Park rangers said he got lost in the woods, died, and wild animals ate him. I don't believe it."

She sucked in a breath at the revelation. That sounded horrible.

"You're not listening to the Skookum stories, are you?" Abe joined their conversation. "Because Fowler will tell you those stories all day."

"That's because they're true, man." Fowler didn't look offended.

"They're his claim to fame in the area. He's our local expert. He even started doing something akin to ghost tours—only with Skookum—here in the summer."

She glanced at Fowler, his story suddenly seeming less reliable. "Is that right?"

"Everyone has to do what they can to make a buck, right? There's no shame in that. Plus, my stories are true. People need to know what these Skookum are capable of."

"I can't argue." Abe turned to her. "Anyway, Boone sent me to come get you. He needs to get your gear fitted."

A rush of nerves fluttered through Brynlee. "Okay, then. Let's do this."

After they left Abe's place, it was already past lunch time. The morning hours had flown by.

Boone and Brynlee walked back toward the town square where most of the festivities were happening and closer to where Boone had parked his truck. He'd had a good talk with Abe and, for a moment, everything had felt normal. Boone had even listened to Brynlee's conversation with Fowler, though he'd tried to pretend like he wasn't paying attention. Fowler had certainly enjoyed sharing his stories and having a captive audience.

He glanced around as he walked—partly to keep an eye out for trouble, and partly just to check out what was going on. More people had turned out as First Friday went into full swing. A local band, Rosie and the Men Who Stole Our Land, played on a nearby stage. He could smell the tantalizing scent of greasy treats cooking from the nearby food trucks.

As he inhaled the aromas, his stomach grumbled. "Please say you want something to eat?"

Brynlee glanced up at him and smiled. "I'd love some food."

"Perfect. Let's go check out what everyone is

offering." They headed toward food truck alley. Those storm clouds were supposed to roll in later. Right now, the air felt brisk but invigorating.

He called hello to several people as they browsed their options. Finally, he settled on some Carolina-style barbecue, and Brynlee grabbed a vegetable wrap with hummus and chips. They sat on a nearby park bench that overlooked Fog Lake to eat.

"So, the people behind me in line were talking about the men who died," Brynlee said as she unwrapped her food and studied it for a minute.

"It's the talk of the town." Boone plucked off a piece of his tangy coleslaw. "People love those trails. They don't want to think about them being dangerous."

"I can see where something like this could shake things up in the area." She took a bite of her wrap, but even that motion didn't conceal her frown.

"You can say that again. Even the trail volunteers don't want to report into work today. I can't say I blame them."

Brynlee leaned back, her wrap still in hand. "Boone, let's say there is a person behind this . . ."

"You mean, someone other than Big Ben?"

"Yes, someone other than Big Ben. Who else might have the motive to do this?"

"Someone crazy." He shrugged and bit into his sandwich. This barbecue was good. Really good.

"But even if it is a crazy person, most likely he will still have a motive or some kind of incident in his background that would lend itself to him doing this, don't you think?"

"I don't know." He looked away from the conversation for a moment to wave at someone from church who walked past. He turned somber again as he turned back to Brynlee. "One thing I've learned in life is that there isn't always a reason for things. We want to believe there is. But that isn't always the case."

"Like with Kat?"

He nodded stiffly as memories tried to pummel him. "Yes, like with Kat. I don't care what anyone says. Her death was senseless."

"I'm sorry, Boone." Brynlee's voice sounded soft with compassion.

"No, it's okay. I usually don't talk about her so much. You're bringing out a different side of me, I suppose." He sighed and glanced at Brynlee. "Who do *you* think might be behind this?"

She shrugged. "You mentioned that Todd man."

"While I don't trust him and I think he has motive, I'm not sure this is the method he would choose for retaliation. Luke is probably right."

"But we know this person is probably familiar with this area, correct?"

He wiped his mouth, still holding his sandwich in his other hand. "Correct."

"He has some kind of connection with wildlife. He at least understands wildlife enough to know how they operate. He knows the trails. He knows the history of the area. The legends."

Boone squinted, trying to follow her train of thought—unsuccessfully. "Okay . . . I'm not sure where you're going with this."

"I'm just trying to put together a mental picture of who this guy might be, if not Big Ben. What could his motive be? Why would he come after me?"

"You haven't been in town for long enough to make any enemies . . . have you?"

"Not that I know of." Her cheeks heated, and she looked away. "I mean, other than that creature in the woods."

"Like I said, maybe this is just a crazy person. Someone without a reason." Boone studied her. "But you can't handle that, can you?"

"I just want things to make sense."

"So what happens when they don't?"

She frowned before quietly saying, "I don't know."

Someone stopped in front of them. Boone looked up and spotted Witherford, the head of the Planning Council. The man had slight features, small glasses, and thinning hair. He took his job very seriously.

"Boone."

Boone nodded. "Witherford."

"I'm glad I ran into you. I thought you should know that we've planned a meeting on Monday to talk about the application for the permit to build on Dead Man's Bluff."

Boone bristled. "Sounds good. I look forward to hashing that out with everyone."

"We can't let this happen, Boone." Witherford stared at Boone, his beady little eyes boring holes into him.

"I don't intend to."

Witherford nodded curtly. "Good. That's what I thought you'd say. I intend to rally support from the other council members to ensure this doesn't happen."

"There's no way the permit will pass. No way."

Witherford nodded at Brynlee. "Have a good day."

After the man walked away, Brynlee leaned toward him. "That man seems intense."

"He is. I think he's even more protective of the mountain than I am."

"Why is that?"

"I have no idea. His family has a long history in

the area, and he wants to preserve it. People around here, we like green space."

"Would a resort on Dead Man's Bluff really be that bad of an idea?"

"It would be a terrible idea. That mountain shouldn't be developed." Boone finished his sandwich, tired of talking about the permit.

As he looked up, he spotted Lonny. The man seemed nice enough, though a touch peculiar. But he remembered the cut on the man's arm.

How had he gotten that? And why did he want to conceal it? Was it because he was somehow involved in all this?

The man was a bear expert.

Then again, what would his motive possibly be? Boone couldn't think of one possible reason why a man like Lonny might be behind these recent attacks.

Maybe he was just looking for a scapegoat. He didn't know.

He balled up his trash and sighed. "Look, I think we should get busy. We need to go over some hiking stuff. Then we need to pack for the hike tomorrow. Right now, the weather is looking good. Let's hope it stays that way."

Just as they stood, screams sounded in the distance.

Boone's muscles tightened as he anticipated

what might be happening. His gut told him it wasn't good.

He looked toward the town square. The crowds ran away from something, panic capturing their features, their motions, their screams.

What in the world was going on?

He sucked in a deep breath as onlookers scattered. There, in the void the crowds had left, stood. . . a Skookum.

27

B rynlee froze, unable to move or tear her gaze away from the scene unfolding. Everyone looked terrified—an emotion she understood well.

As she saw the furry creature who'd stirred the fear, her stomach flip-flopped. He looked crazy. Rabid. Out of control as he flailed his arms in the air and another growl emerged from him.

Boone reached for her arm and pushed Brynlee behind him. His muscles bristled as he stood on guard, clearly ready to protect her.

The realization filled her heart with a strange comfort. She'd never known what it was like to have someone look out for her. But Brynlee reminded herself again that he was only doing this because she was paying him. No other reason.

Her gaze remained focused on the creature in the distance. He lifted his hands again, his sharp claws glistening in the sunlight. His body was crouched, like he was just looking for someone to pounce on.

More people screamed and ran away in a panic.

Then the creature stopped.

Paused.

Look around.

His body bent forward.

Bent forward?

Brynlee held her breath, waiting to see what would happen next.

The next instant, the creature put his hands on his neck . . . and pulled off a mask.

A mask?

Wait . . . that was a man in a costume?

Her shoulders slumped.

A teenager's laughing face appeared.

This had been a joke. Irritation pounded inside her.

In front of her, Boone's shoulders tightened. She could feel the testiness rising off him as he glared at the teen in the distance.

"Stay here," he barked.

He charged through the crowd and took the teenager by the arm. His other hand was on his phone, which was already at his ear.

No doubt he was calling Luke.

That teenager had probably done this as a joke. But someone could have gotten hurt or the teen could have even been shot. It was in poor taste considering everything that had happened in town.

Brynlee dropped back onto the bench, her vegetable wrap nearly forgotten now. The crowds seemed to hesitantly return to their activities. The band began playing again, but this time a ballad that seemed to reflect the change of mood at this First Friday event.

Boone paused in front of Brynlee. He still gripped the agitated teenager. The boy tried to pull out of his grasp and muttered under his breath that people couldn't take a joke.

Boone scowled and ignored him. "I need to take him down to the sheriff's office."

"If it's okay, I'll wait here," Brynlee said. "I need to return a couple phone calls."

His eyes narrowed, like he was unsure. "Are you positive?"

"Yeah, I'm positive. I'm in public. I should be okay."

Finally, he nodded, though he still looked hesitant. "I should be only a few minutes."

As soon as he was out of earshot, Brynlee called the surveyor she'd hired to access the property.

She'd been waiting for a moment alone to check in with Stephen Royce.

He wasn't supposed to actually have to hike the mountainside. She'd warned him about what had happened. She just needed him to use his drone to get a better idea of the property around Dead Man's Bluff.

He didn't answer.

She frowned. Didn't answer? Stephen was okay, right?

Maybe his cell phone was just out of range. Surely, he'd call her as soon as he finished.

But a bad feeling remained in Brynlee's stomach. Maybe Boone was right and that mountain was nothing but trouble.

Nearly as soon as they drove into Boone's driveway, Brynlee's phone rang.

She hoped it was Stephen.

Instead she saw Mason's number. Mason, her half-brother. Why in the world would he be calling her?

She excused herself, climbed from the truck, and stepped away from Boone. "Hello, Mason."

"Hello, Brynlee," he said.

"Why are you calling?" There was no need to

beat around the bush. He'd never called her before just for friendly conversation, so he obviously had a reason now.

"How are things in Fog Lake?"

"How did you know I was in Fog Lake?" Brynlee's suspicions rose. She hadn't told him she was coming here.

"I'm on the board for my father's company. I know what's going on. I know what his last wishes were."

"Then I guess you know how things are going here also, don't you?"

He let out a sigh. "Look, I'm not sure you realize how much opposition Dad received last time he tried this."

"I'm aware. He told me."

"I think it's a bad plan to be there right now."

Brynlee glanced at Boone and saw that he was busy setting up the climbing equipment. "I'll be the judge of that. Now, is this really why you called?"

"Yes, this is really why I called. To warn you. I don't want to see anything bad happen to you while you're there."

Her muscles tightened. Did he know about the men who died? About everything that had happened to her? If so, how?

He wouldn't be so desperate for his father's

money that he'd use this as an excuse to harm her . . . would he?

As crazy as the thought sounded, she couldn't dismiss it. People did crazy things for money.

Maybe even going as far as capitalizing on the killings in the mountains and trying to bring the legend of the Skookum to life . . .

28

Boone and Brynlee spent the rest of the day in his backyard practicing how to use ropes and rappelling and belaying. There was a small rock wall there they could use. Brynlee wasn't what he'd call a natural. No, she now had scrapes on the palms of her hands, and she'd even torn her jeans. But this was the best place to learn.

Though he doubted Brynlee was going to be great at doing any of this, he had to admire her willingness to see this crazy dream through to fruition.

Afterward, they went to Luke and Harper's place. Harper had fixed dinner—a vegetable pasta dish that was delicious. It felt surprisingly normal for all of them to eat together. And Brynlee fit in surprisingly well.

Why did that bring Boone a small measure of delight?

Once Luke and Harper turned in for the evening, Boone and Brynlee remained on the couch, close enough that their knees touched when they turned toward each other.

Boone felt thankful for a few minutes to talk to her alone and get a feel for how she was doing and what she was thinking. His breath caught when he looked at her. Earlier, she'd changed into some yoga pants and a sweatshirt. Her makeup was gone, and her hair was pulled back into a ponytail.

She'd never looked more beautiful.

Boone cleared his throat, which had started to feel unreasonably achy. "Are you sure you're up for this?"

Brynlee tucked her legs beneath her and nodded. "I am."

He leaned back into the couch and drew in a deep breath, feeling himself starting to unwind—even if just a little. It was good to get away from the craziness for a few minutes.

He had the strange desire to talk to her, not as someone who'd been thrown into this situation with her, but as a person.

"So, tell me about your dad. Why was going up to Dead Man's Bluff his dream?"

She glanced at her hands, her earlier lightheartedness disappearing. "It's a long story but . . . the truth is that I didn't even know my dad existed until about fourteen months ago."

He waited for her to continue or to tell him to mind his own business.

"I told you earlier that my mom was a singer. Apparently, my mom and dad met while she was on the road, and they fell in love—quickly. My mom was a bit of gypsy spirit, and my dad wanted to settle down, so they went their separate ways. Then she found out she was pregnant. But she . . . she never told my dad, apparently."

Boone bit back a frown. "What did she tell you when you were old enough to ask?"

Brynlee rubbed her lips together, her eyes glazing as if she'd drifted to another time. "She told me that my dad had died before I was born, but that he was a wonderful man and I would have loved him. I had no reason to think she lied to me."

"So, how did you figure it out?"

She shrugged. "To backtrack a little . . . my mom and I were on the road all the time. I basically home-schooled myself. And I hated that life. I wanted stability. I wanted consistency. Instead, I was at a new place almost every night."

"I'm sure that was difficult." Boone imagined Brynlee as a child. Imagined her alone and neglected while her mom was out following the dream of making it as a singer. His heart went out to Brynlee. It couldn't have been an easy way to grow up.

"It was difficult. But I finished high school. I'd always loved making things look nice, so I decided to go to college and get my degree in art. I quickly figured out that world wasn't for me, so I went back and studied interior design instead. I was designing a client's house when I got the call that my mom had died in a car accident."

"That's terrible."

"It was. Despite our differences, I think my mom loved me deep down inside. And I don't ever remember feeling as alone as I did after she passed. I felt like it was me against the world." Brynlee sucked in a deep breath and absently picked at some imaginary lint.

"I know that must have been hard for you."

Finally, Brynlee looked up again, a new glimmer in her eyes. "And then one day I got a phone call from a man named Samuel. He told me he did a DNA test, and it had come back that we were related. I thought it was a joke."

"I didn't think things like that happened in real life." Boone had certainly heard some stories but, honestly, he'd doubted their authenticity.

"I didn't either. I was very skeptical. A friend had gotten me one of those ancestry kits for Christmas, but I didn't think anything would come of it. Especially nothing like finding my father."

"What did you do?"

"After a few texts back and forth, I figured it couldn't hurt to meet this man somewhere public. It turned out he lived only two hours away from my house in Pennsylvania. As soon as I saw him . . . I knew he was telling the truth. We looked so much alike. He was my dad."

Boone draped an arm across the back of the couch. He had the urge to pull her into an embrace but didn't, despite the impulse. "Why would your mom lie to you all those years?"

"She was afraid that if my dad knew I was alive, he would try to take me from her. My dad was a successful businessman and had much more means than my mom did. He had stability. She knew the odds would be against her, especially if social services ever found out how I was living."

Boone's heart panged. Maybe he'd misjudged Brynlee. She wasn't Ms. LL Bean—a spoiled rich girl who was used to getting what she wanted. He regretted the assumption.

"Did you and your dad hit it off?" he asked.

"Yes, you could say that. But it was just a little too late. He'd been diagnosed with congestive heart failure and was living on borrowed time. He'd been married—and divorced—and he had three sons. He said he'd always wanted a daughter. We bonded right away, and I spent as much time with him as I could. I really enjoyed getting to know him and learning from him, even if it was for a short period."

"That's good, at least."

"It was good. While we were talking, he told me about his time in Fog Lake and how much he loved it. He made me promise I'd see Dead Man's Bluff for myself and that I'd scatter some of his ashes there. He said I'd never be the same afterward."

"That's a great story, Brynlee." His hand brushed her hair. He resisted the temptation to run his fingers through the strands. Resisted the urge to playfully tug her ponytail.

"Yeah, it is pretty great—most of it, at least. I mean, he died four months ago. I'm so glad I got to meet him, but I do wish we'd had more time."

"At least you're able to honor his wishes now."

She nodded and glanced at her hands in her lap again. Her voice sounded wistful as she said, "Yeah, at least there's that."

Without thinking, Boone reached over, took her hand, and squeezed.

Brynlee glanced up, an almost shy look in her eyes as she smiled at him.

Something about the moment bonded them. Or maybe it was this situation. Whatever it was, Boone felt the walls around his heart slowly breaking down.

Brynlee felt all her insides turning gooey.

She should not be having this reaction to Boone Wilder. Not to Boone Wilder who infuriated her.

But there was something about him that seemed so tender right now. As she glanced at his green eyes, she felt as if she could see into his soul.

She didn't ever remember feeling like that before.

She cleared her throat and leaned back. "You know, my mom wrote a song about me once."

She'd clearly changed the subject, but how could she not? She needed something to distract her.

"Did she? What kind of song?"

"It was a ballad about what she wanted for my future."

"Can you sing it for me?"

She let out a laugh. "I don't sing."

"Then tell me what the song was about."

She pushed a strand of hair behind her ear as she remembered her mom singing the lyrics. Her mom had loved her, but she'd never been a great mom. She'd been so focused on her career that Brynlee had always been an afterthought.

While most children spent their childhood playing with friends at the park, Brynlee had spent her childhood listening to her mom warm up at bars. During the concerts themselves, Brynlee had usually escaped to the RV that would be parked behind the building.

She'd had no consistent friends or family or school even.

Brynlee cleared her throat. "It was about how she hoped I had the life that she never did."

"What did that mean?"

"It meant that she chased empty dreams. She was always alone. When she wasn't alone, she was with someone who didn't mean anything to her. People admired her, but only a few people knew her."

"It sounds . . . sad."

"I guess her life was full of highs and lows. The highs of getting the gigs she hoped for. The lows of never really going anywhere or having anything to show for it."

"She had you."

Brynlee shrugged. "Maybe. I mean, I loved my mom. But . . . if I have kids one day, it's not the kind of childhood I would wish on them."

"That's the nice part about life, isn't it? The ability to choose our own paths?"

"Yeah, I guess it is." She realized how personal

she'd gotten and knew she needed to veer onto a safer subject. "Boone, about the hike tomorrow—"

He sucked in a deep breath when she mentioned it. "I've been thinking about it all day. Everyone seems confident that between Big Ben and this bear they've captured that we should be safe."

"Is it a risk we should take?" She didn't want to be stupid here. She really didn't.

"When you put all the evidence together, it does look like a closed case, doesn't it?"

Brynlee nodded. "Yeah, it does."

"If this is still what you want to do, then we can go for it."

She smiled. "Okay, then. It's a plan."

Brynlee really, really hoped they didn't regret this. She and Boone were both trusting the conclusions of the experts here. But why did Brynlee have to wonder if the experts might be wrong?

29

His instincts were finely tuned.

But he didn't even need to use them today. No, all about town Brynlee and her "security guard" had spoken of their plans to climb Dead Man's Bluff the next day.

Could they make it any easier for him?

Besides, they had no idea who he was. He'd been out and about in Fog Lake, in plain sight, and they had no idea. The two of them were practically stupid little sheep, not having any clue.

He'd expected more from Boone Wilder. But the man had no idea what he was up against. The camping store owner still thought a bear was behind this and that Big Ben was involved.

A smile stretched across his face.

Both Boone and Brynlee were as jumpy as fleas on a rabid dog.

He couldn't wait to put an end to their plan. He couldn't wait to show them they didn't have any power.

He stood behind the trees again, this time in the woods beside the home of Luke and Harper Wilder. No one would see him out here in the dark, and he felt no fear at being discovered. He practically felt untouchable right now.

Through the window, he saw Boone and Brynlee. Saw them talking on the couch. Saw the bond that was developing between them.

As he watched them, the hunger returned. The hunger for blood. He could taste it now. He craved it.

No, there are other ways.

He shook his head and stared at his prey through the window again. The notion that tried to claim him wasn't true. This was the only way to stop Brynlee Parker and her plan to destroy this area.

Soon, Boone would find out. Soon everything would crumble.

He watched for another moment. The two of them smiled on the couch. Boone touched Brynlee's hand. They were more than bonding. They were becoming fond of each other.

That wouldn't last long.

A smile spread across his face.

He couldn't wait to see everything come to a violent end.

30

The next morning, Brynlee glanced around the mountainside, praying this wasn't her worst idea ever. She prayed the side of her mom that Brynlee had always despised wasn't becoming one of her own traits. The side that didn't think things through. The side that was irresponsible and driven to do things that weren't in anyone's best interests but her own.

Her stomach clenched at the thought. Then again, maybe she was acting more like her dad—driven to the point of having her blinders on to anything else. Just like her father had been clueless to the fact that he had a daughter.

For that matter, what if she'd been given the worst characteristics of both her mom and dad?

She pushed those thoughts aside, knowing it

would do no good to dwell on them now. They would only slow her down.

She and Boone had already been hiking for three hours. The first hour, just as on her previous trek up, had been fairly easy. The second hour had become considerably steeper. The third hour it was both steep and rocky.

They'd eaten some snacks as they walked, knowing they couldn't waste any time and that they needed to keep their energy levels up. But the peanut butter wasn't settling well in her stomach now.

Boone had warned her that soon they would be walking on something called the Razor Back. It was a narrow ridge with steep drop-offs on either side. He said Brynlee would feel like she was walking on the back of a dinosaur.

So far, there had been no incidents—only peace and quiet. Brynlee was tired, winded, and her legs hurt, but, overall, she felt invigorated instead of exhausted. Maybe she could be more of an outdoor girl than she thought.

And Boone had been surprisingly good company. He'd told her stories of growing up in this area, of what it was like to have Luke for an older brother and the town sheriff as a father. He told her about Ansley and his younger brother, Jaxon, who was serving in the Middle East right now.

He looked like a natural out here. He might have joked about her being Ms. LL Bean—yes, she'd heard his nickname for her—but Boone made for one handsome outdoorsman in his jeans, hiking boots, and thick jacket. His stocking cap covered his ears, but curls crept out from beneath it. His five o'clock shadow made him look rugged and surprisingly stylish—even though she was sure that wasn't the look he was going for.

All of that mixed with his mischievous green eyes and fun-loving spirit made for an enticing total package.

Brynlee had almost forgotten just how hard this hike was.

Almost.

As Boone paused in front of her, she glanced ahead. The trail was changing again. She could feel it.

She glanced beyond Boone, and her thoughts were confirmed.

The trees cleared, and a mountain ridge stretched in front of them. She sucked in a deep breath, already feeling lightheaded at the thought of walking across the Razor Back. But it was either the Razor Back or scale the cliff.

She'd take the Razor Back.

But it was narrow. It was steep on either side. And the path itself was rocky.

"This is it." Boone stood in front of her like a conqueror with his hands on his hips. "We've been averaging two miles an hour. We should reach Dead Man's Bluff in about thirty minutes."

"We're that close?"

He pointed in the distance. "There it is, right there."

Brynlee stared at the vista ahead. It was breathtaking. At the end of the Razor Back area was something that almost looked like an island in the sky.

Dead Man's Bluff.

The whole area was rocky but dotted with patches of green. Clouds floated beneath it. A lone tree grew there, perched on the edge of the landscape.

She'd never seen anything like it before. "It's . . . everything I thought it would be . . . and more."

"A lot of people have that reaction."

"So that's the cliff that some people climb to get to Dead Man's Bluff?" She pointed to a rock face on the other side of Dead Man's Bluff that looked intimidating, to say the least.

"That's right. Going that way does cut off some distance, but it's nowhere near as safe."

She stared at the path in front of her, feeling a trickle of nerves. "I think this is challenging enough."

"We've climbed about three thousand feet in

elevation since we left this morning. There's an entirely different weather system up here. It can be sunny down in Fog Lake, but up here a storm can blow in at a moment's notice."

"That would explain why we passed through some clouds earlier. And the change of temperature. It's downright cold up here."

He flashed a smile at her, as if this conversation entertained him. "Yes, it is. You ready to finish this?"

"Ready as I'll ever be."

Boone locked gazes with her, as if sensing her anxiety. "Just keep this in mind: whatever you focus on is where you'll go."

"What do you mean?"

"I mean, if you look at the drop-off, you'll be more likely to head toward the drop-off. But if you keep focused on the steps that you need to take to reach your destination, you'll be much more surefooted."

His words washed over Brynlee on more than one level. "Sounds like good advice."

"I've got some in me sometimes." He blew on his fingers and rubbed them against his shirt in fake humility.

"That's good to know." She smiled. "Okay, let's do this. Let's go see Dead Man's Bluff and see what all the fuss is about."

Boone surveyed the area in front of him, still perplexed as to why he was actually on this trail. He hadn't been up here since . . . well, since Katherine. Memories tried to push themselves up, but he continually shoved them back down.

This was not the time to let emotions get in his way or to let memories bog him down. He'd have time for that later.

He'd packed the supplies they needed into backpacks, taken one for himself and given the other to Brynlee. If they stayed on course, they'd be back at the trailhead by sunset. The timing would work out perfectly.

He could tell Brynlee was tired, but she pressed on. They had little choice for a trip like this. It would easily take five hours to get up the mountain and five hours to get back down. They needed to operate during daylight hours in order to remain safe.

Since it was March, they had only ten hours of daylight.

That meant, they had no time to waste.

As he continued to navigate the path, his mind went back to Katherine.

She loved this trail. Loved this mountain. Loved this town.

Sometimes, it still seemed surreal that she was

gone. They'd been together for seven years, and only married for one day. Losing her . . . it had been the hardest thing he'd ever gone through.

Harder than his dad's cancer diagnosis.

Harder than his mom walking out when she couldn't handle the "for worse" part of marriage.

Harder than seeing his sister turn into a totally different person in the aftermath of everything. As he'd told Brynlee yesterday, sometimes there wasn't a reason. Sometimes, things just were.

He glanced back at Brynlee as she climbed over the rocks, looking uncertain. She crouched, like she might have to grab onto something and hold on for dear life. He fought a smile.

"How are you doing back there?" he asked.

"Looking forward," Brynlee said.

"Isn't that all we can do?" As soon as the words left Boone's mouth, he realized he should take his own advice. He'd been living in the past for too long.

He reached the end of the Razor Back area.

They were almost there now. Only a little distance longer.

He glanced behind him again and watched Brynlee as she climbed toward him. Watched her blonde hair that fell to her shoulders in glossy waves. Saw the determination in both her eyes and in her motions.

Brynlee was nothing like Katherine.

Katherine had been all natural. No makeup. No fancy hairdos.

She'd like things around her neat, but she'd never cared about decorating her home or making things look nice.

Then there was Brynlee. She loved making things more welcoming. She was sensitive to what others thought, it seemed. She was focused, but she also had a softer side.

Boone reached out his hand to her. "Come on. Let's do this together."

She looked up, a grateful smile on her face mixing with satisfaction as the summit came into sight. "Sounds like a plan."

Brynlee reached up and grabbed Boone's outstretched hand. Her fingers caught in his grip, and he pulled her up to the end of the trail—to the top of the summit.

To Dead Man's Bluff, the famed site that so many hikers sought to reach.

She sucked in a quick breath as she took that final step. Instead of glancing around, she needed to breathe. The journey had winded her.

It had been much, much more difficult than she'd thought. Yoga and running a 5K hadn't been the training she needed, by any stretch of the imagination. Walking the Razor Back had been invigorating.

Finally, she pulled herself up to full height. The ground was pure rock beneath her feet. But she felt like king of the hill.

As she glanced around, a gasp escaped. This time it wasn't from exhaustion, but amazement.

"This view . . ." she whispered, unable to pull her eyes away. "It's amazing."

"Isn't it?"

They stood beside each other and gazed out over the scene around them. Mountains rolled for miles upon miles. The blue and black tops blended together. Fluffy clouds lay below them, blanketing everything with a smoky look—the one that had given this area its very name.

"People say you can see North Carolina, South Carolina, and Georgia from here," Boone said.

"It's unlike anything I've ever seen."

"It used to be my favorite place." A hint of sadness saturated his voice.

Brynlee squeezed her arm, somehow understanding his pain. Desperately wishing she could help him. But so grateful he was here with her now.

She turned and looked in the other direction. Her throat tightened at what she saw. The summit actually had probably twenty acres of surprisingly flat land . . . land that would nicely accommodate some sort of attraction where other people could enjoy this fabulous view. It was perfect . . . just like her father had told her.

Speaking of her father . . . she didn't have much time left up here. She pulled his ashes from her bag. Her heart twisted as she unscrewed the top and held out the cannister. Silently, Boone joined her.

"Fly free, Dad," she whispered. "I wish we'd had more time together. One day."

Without saying anything more, Brynlee turned the cannister and watched his ashes float over the cliffside, mingling with the wind, and being carried over the mountain.

Boone squeezed her arm. "You okay?"

Solemnly, she nodded. "Yeah, I am."

As they stood there a few more minutes, Boone didn't rush her. She honored her dad's memory with a moment of silence.

When she felt satisfied, she turned to Boone. "I guess we should go."

"Can I show you something first?" Boone's gaze searched hers, his green eyes showing depths of emotions that Brynlee hadn't expected.

"Of course."

He took her arm and tugged her to the old oak tree that grew near the edge of the cliff. The tree was striking as it dramatically drove its roots down over the side of the mountain. Yet, despite its position, it still looked strong.

"It's unusual to have a tree like this at such a high elevation," Boone said. "And that's just one of the many reasons I've always loved this tree. It's different. It's withstood time, elements, and expectations. And it's beautiful."

"It is gorgeous."

Boone stopped in front of the tree and leaned around to the far side. He squatted there and pointed at something on the bark. "Look at this."

She peered beside him and saw little tally marks there. It was interesting, she supposed, but she had a feeling there was more to the story.

Boone ran his finger down each mark. "There are twelve marks. One for each time Katherine and I reached the summit together."

"That's really sweet," Brynlee said. She envied the relationship they'd had. Boone had obviously cared about her deeply. She longed for affection like that in her own life.

Above the spot were the words "Boone + Kat 4ever."

Brynlee smiled bittersweetly. What a tragic loss.

And then she paused. "Boone, didn't you say you haven't been up since she died?"

"That's right. Why?"

She double-checked what she was about to say.

She needed to be absolutely certain before she voiced her thoughts out loud.

She nodded, certain now but dreading the firestorm of emotions her words might set in motion.

"Boone, there are thirteen marks on the tree."

31

Boone leaned closer and counted the tally marks again. Brynlee was right.

There were thirteen marks on the tree.

His heart thudded a beat as a realization he didn't want to solidify began to take definite shape.

What if . . . what if Katherine had made it up here? What if the story, as he knew it, hadn't been correct for all these years?

Everything seemed to fade around him.

"What are you thinking?" Brynlee asked, her voice soft and prodding as she knelt beside him.

As the question resounded in his head, he frowned, still trying to come to terms with the conclusion his mind drew. He shook his head and wiped a hand down his face. "I don't know."

She remained beside him, not saying anything.

Boone appreciated the quiet. His thoughts were loud enough.

"She made it up here, Brynlee." Boone touched the last tally mark and imagined Kat triumphantly putting it there.

"Does that change things?"

"Yeah, that changes everything." His voice faded to a whisper.

Brynlee studied his face. "What do you mean?"

"I mean, everyone thought Kat's rope broke, and she fell below." His voice cracked as the truth slammed into him. "But if she reached the top, she would have no reason to go back down."

"Maybe she wanted you to think you won."

"No, she wasn't the type." A sad smile crossed his lips as her image captured his mind. The sparkle in her eyes. The determined set of her muscles. The lilt of her voice as excitement set in. "She liked to win and showed no mercy."

"Then . . ."

Boone's gaze locked with Brynlee's. "Then I think she made it up here, and something else happened to her. I think someone else made it look like she'd been in a tragic accident."

Brynlee looked like she was hardly breathing, and her voice sounded wispy as she asked, "Why would someone do that?"

He shook his head, a rock in his chest. "I have no idea. But I need to find out."

"I'm sorry, Boone." Compassion stained the words and as she laid a hand on his back, he nearly broke.

"Me too." His mind whirled through the facts. What if Kat's death hadn't been an accident at all? What if it had been staged to look like that? Even worse —what if the person responsible was still at large?

His mind raced, and his grief turned into thirst for justice.

As he glanced at Brynlee, he realized they needed to move. This wasn't the time to freeze or mourn or even get angry. No, there were too many other things on the line.

As he saw the sun beginning to sink, he frowned. "We need to get back before it gets dark."

"If you're ready to leave."

"Yeah." His voice sounded hoarse, despite his resolve not to let this realization affect his logic.

With one last glance at the tree, he stepped toward the Razor Back trail. Just as he took the first step, his phone rang. He paused.

He couldn't believe he actually had reception out here. He glanced at his screen and saw it was Luke. If he was calling, he probably had a good reason.

"What's going on?" Boone answered.

"Where are you, Boone?" Luke sounded serious, his voice urgent on the other end.

"I'm at Dead Man's Bluff. Why?"

"You need to get off that mountain. Now."

He bristled, bracing himself for whatever his brother was about to say. "What's going on?"

"We just found another dead body. The man appears to have died this morning . . . after we'd caught that bear and after Big Ben was arrested."

Brynlee watched Boone's expression. She'd heard the change in his voice and knew something had happened. As soon as he put his phone away, she asked, "What is it? What happened?"

"Someone else was killed this morning."

"You mean . . . this thing is still out there?" Brynlee felt breathless as she said the words. This couldn't be true. Couldn't be happening. Someone else dead?

"That's how it looks." Boone's jaw clenched as he stared down at her, the Razor Back trail stretching behind him like an ominous warning.

Brynlee's head swirled with such force that she backed up and lowered herself onto a boulder. Her lungs felt tight, and fear nearly crackled in the air.

"I . . . what . . ." She couldn't find her words. "What are we going to do?"

Boone's eyes locked with hers, his gaze unwavering. "We're going to have to get back to safety. We knew this was a risk when we came out here."

The thought of being immersed in those woods with that creature . . . it caused a wave of panic to shudder through her. "But—"

Boone stepped closer and bent closer toward her. "There's no other way, Brynlee. Vehicles can't get up here. It's too cloudy for a helicopter. Not enough space for a plane. We have no choice but to hike back down."

Terror seemed to numb both her muscles and her thoughts.

She didn't want to be in those woods. She didn't want to be anywhere near that creature. She craved the safety of her condo back in Pennsylvania. Of her favorite blanket. Of a warm cup of coffee.

Out here, she felt exposed. Without a safety net. Without . . . hope.

Boone knelt down closer until they were nearly eye to eye. "It's going to be okay. We're going to do this."

"How?" Her voice trembled. "He'll kill us, Boone. You know he will. He could be following us now."

Using a finger, Boone nudged her chin up. "That's not going to happen."

She wanted to believe his words. She really did. But . . . "You haven't seen him. You don't know what he's capable of."

He lowered his voice. "Brynlee, I'm going to need you to give everything you've got on this hike back down. I know you can do it. It's going to be hard. Scary. And it's going to test everything you've got."

How did she tell him that she never remembered being this terrified in all her life? That she felt paralyzed, like she was living a nightmare?

"We need to get going, okay?" Boone continued, sounding like a negotiator trying to talk someone off the ledge.

The urge to throw up gripped Brynlee even more fiercely. But she pushed it down. This had been her idea. Her plan. She'd gotten them into this. Now she had to be strong and find courage she didn't know she had.

"Okay," she said. "Let's go."

But why did she feel like she was hiking the green mile—the walk to her final destination?

Because this creature had targeted her. And she knew beyond a doubt that this was far from being over.

32

Brynlee's thoughts raced as she stared at the Razor Back. Coming up had been one thing. Going down . . . it looked a whole lot scarier. And now her nerves were shot.

This had been a stupid idea to come out here. She should have listened to Boone.

The problem had been that she didn't have that much time. She'd said she'd be back in Pennsylvania by next week. As much as she'd like to stay longer and enjoy this area, it wasn't possible.

For that matter, maybe she *was* exactly like her mom.

"You can do this," Boone repeated. "Remember, focus on where you're going, where you'll step next. Don't look down."

"Okay." If only Brynlee felt so certain.

"I'll be here if you need me."

Brynlee took a few more tentative steps as she followed Boone.

She'd heard about the bear being captured, about Big Ben being arrested . . . she'd figured with the two of them gone, she was safe. Both the beast and the man portion of her fears had been covered.

She took another step and reminded herself to breathe.

Maybe if she'd looked more deeply inside herself, maybe she would have realized that neither had felt right in her gut. She'd wanted to believe it . . . but that didn't mean she should have.

And now she'd put Boone in danger as well.

Despair rumbled in her stomach.

If anything happened, this would be her fault.

Brynlee crept forward, unable to stop looking over the edge. At the emptiness below. At the hundreds of feet she could fall without anything to stop her. Boone might not say it, but Brynlee knew that one wrong move, and she'd plunge to her death.

As she glanced down again, her head swirled. She felt like she was losing her balance.

She paused and glanced up. The sun had begun its descent. They had to make it back to Fog Lake before dark. There was no other option.

She took several more steps and then froze as she reached the narrowest part of the trail.

This had been her least favorite part on the way up. She'd never loved heights. She didn't tell Boone that. She could already tell he didn't want to be here, and she didn't want to add any more fuel to the fire.

"You ready for this?" Boone asked.

"As ready as I'll ever be." She took another step and nearly plummeted as a rock tumbled beneath her feet. She caught herself by lowering herself to the ground until she had her balance. But her heart raced out of control.

Boone paused in front of her. "How about if I set up this rope as a safety? Just to be on the cautious side."

A safety net? Nothing sounded better. But . . . "Do we have time?"

"We're going to have to make time for it." He took his pack off and pulled out one of the ropes.

Brynlee wasn't sure what he was thinking, but Boone moved like a man with a mission. She watched him with curiosity as he expertly began tying knots.

But she watched more than that.

She observed the pain in his eyes. The pain of knowing that his wife had made it to the top. That there was more to her death than he'd ever assumed. What a horrible realization.

Was that somehow tied in with what was going

on now? She had a hard time seeing how it would
be. It had to be a terrible coincidence . . . right?

Boone finished and hooked up her harness.

"Okay, you're good to go," he said. "Just take your
time. If anything happens, this will catch you. I'll be
there as well."

She felt lightheaded as she continued. One
wrong move and . . .

Against her better senses, she glanced down
again. Steep drop-offs fell on both sides of her. What
was that? Two hundred feet? She'd plunge to her
death if she wasn't careful.

No, Brynlee had her safety line. She touched her
harness to make sure she hadn't imagined any of
this. She hadn't.

She just had to keep moving.

"I'll be right behind you," Boone said. "Just take
your time."

The problem was, Brynlee knew they didn't have
time. That beast . . . creature . . . man . . . he was still
out here. The sooner they were off this mountain,
the better.

"You see that foothold right there?" Boone
pointed to a rock that jutted out an inch or two. "See
if you can reach it. It will be easier going after that.
You'll have a good five inches of ledge."

Five inches? She needed five feet to feel comfortable . . . if even that would work.

Her hands trembled as she took her first step. She closed her eyes, lifted a prayer, and then reached for another foothold. As her toes hit it, she released her breath.

She'd done it. Now she just needed to pull the rest of her body over.

Taking a deep breath, she shifted her weight.

As she did, the ledge beneath her gave way.

She felt herself sliding down to a certain death below.

Boone heard the rock crumble only a split second before Brynlee slipped from the trail.

He jerked his arm out and caught her—but barely. His muscles strained, and he tried to balance himself there on the ledge.

Brynlee dangled below, her eyes wide orbs of terror.

Her safety line had caught her. She was secure. But she was also terrified.

"I've got you," Boone said.

No sooner had the words left his lips than he heard something snap.

"Boone!" Brynlee yelled.

His gaze darted toward Brynlee. As it did, his arm jerked with an unanticipated weight.

What . . . ?

And then he saw it. Brynlee's line had broken.

Flashbacks of Katherine hit him again. Her final moments. How scared and alone she must have felt.

The thoughts snapped him back into action.

"You're going to be okay," he told Brynlee.

Her weight pulled him downward, and Boone had little to hold onto. There was nothing here but loose rocks. The situation was precarious—but he wouldn't tell Brynlee that.

Certainly, she already knew anyway.

The rocks beneath him shifted, and he reached for something to grab onto. There was nothing.

They both dropped two feet until their feet hit another ledge.

A gasped half scream escaped from Brynlee.

"I've got you," he told her through gritted teeth. "Can you find a foothold?"

"I'll try."

Boone watched as she seemed to feel around with her feet. She didn't dare look down. Finally, she must have found a small ledge. Some of the weight left his arm.

Still, this was going to be harder than he thought. At least his line was still holding.

But for how long?

Boone didn't feel certain he could trust it.

"I'm going to pull you back up, okay?" Boone said.

"Okay." Brynlee's voice trembled as she stared up at him, desperation in her gaze.

Using every last ounce of his energy, he pulled her toward him. "Grab on to the ledge," he told her through gritted teeth.

One of her hands released from his, and she grasped on to the rock facing.

Boone let out a breath.

Now he just needed to help her pull herself the rest of the way up.

As he reached for Brynlee, his line caught slack.

They both began to slide down the cliff again.

Boone's belt rubbed against the rocky mountainside. Something snapped.

He glanced down and saw his gun clattering down the rock face.

He held his breath as he watched it slip out of reach.

"What is it?" Brynlee asked, her entire body tense and dread in her eyes. She still didn't dare look down, though.

Smart girl.

"My gun . . . it came out of the holster as I was sliding."

"Can you reach it?"

Boone stared at it down below. He couldn't reach

it easily, that was for sure. Was it even worth it? It would take so much time—time they didn't have. Yet to not have a weapon when they were in these woods . . . his stomach clenched at the thought. It left him literally between a rock and a hard place.

He sighed. "I don't think so. Right now, we need to concentrate on getting you to safety."

She nodded nervously. "What do I need to do?"

"We're both going to have to climb back up to the trail."

"I'm scared, Boone." Her voice trembled as she said the words.

"I know. But you can do this. My line will hold us up." As soon as Boone said the words, he heard another snap.

His safety line had broken also.

33

Brynlee barely held back her scream as she saw Boone sliding down the steep mountainside.

He wasn't going to stop, was he?

But as soon as the thought entered her mind, Boone jerked to a halt.

He caught himself by his fingertips, she realized.

She released her breath. But this wasn't over. Far from it.

Still gripping the rock facing, she ignored her lightheadedness and stared down at Boone. "Are you okay?"

"I've been better." Boone grimaced as he looked up at her. "This just got a little harder."

"I just want to get off this Razor Back area," she murmured, trying to control her fear.

It wasn't working.

Every time she looked down, her head began to spin.

It was a long way to the bottom . . . a trip she knew she wouldn't survive. Neither would Boone.

"You're going to have to listen to me," Boone said from below her. "I want you to find all the footholds and handholds you can. You're going to climb back to the top of the Razor Back."

"I don't know if I can do that." The thought of it caused cold fear to shoot through her veins. As she sucked in another breath, cool air filled her lungs.

The temperature was starting to drop even more.

Time was not on their side right now.

"Of course you can," Boone said. Even as he hung on by his fingertips below her, his eyes still had an unwavering confidence that beckoned her to believe in herself. "You can do anything you set your mind to."

"Are you a motivational speaker in your free time?" Brynlee tried to add some lightness to the situation. But her chuckle sounded fake, even to her own ears.

"I was trying not to say anything, but you found me out." As Boone said the words, he began climbing, moving skillfully up the cliff.

How could he do that? One wrong move and . . . he had nothing to catch him.

Her amazement for the man grew.

"What do I need to do?" she asked, a new determination rising in her.

"You're going to grab that handhold right there." He nodded toward the spot. "And put your foot on that ledge. You're going to pull yourself up."

"I don't know if I can." She stared up at the area, at where she needed to go.

"Do I need to bring out my motivational speaker side again?" Boone's voice contained a gentle humor.

"No, no. You're right. I can do this." Brynlee remembered that determination and courage she needed to tap into.

She lifted up a prayer before doing as Boone said. As she put her weight on the rock facing, she held her breath, expecting it to crumble beneath her again.

It didn't.

"Good girl," Boone said. He was nearly beside her now. He'd moved effortlessly to reach her. Fearlessly. "Now you just need to do that again. Keep moving up."

He directed her on where to step. Brynlee followed everything he said closely, not daring to make a wrong move.

Finally, her feet hit the top of the Razor Back, and she nearly collapsed there.

She was safe. For a moment, at least.

Boone climbed up behind her and let out a long breath, his shoulders seeming to slump with relief.

She wished the worst of this was over. But she knew the Skookum was still out there. And they still had a long journey ahead.

Boone's thoughts raced as they continued down the trail. They'd lost a significant amount of time during that fiasco.

What had happened to the climbing equipment? How could it have failed them both? It made no sense.

He tried to recall when it had been out of his sight after he picked it up yesterday. But he couldn't remember any time when someone else could have tampered with it. It had been fine last night when he and Brynlee had used it outside in his backyard.

But right now his primary focus was getting them out of these woods. They were almost halfway back to the trailhead—but that meant they'd still have nearly another hour and a half until they reached the end. A lot could happen in that time.

Boone didn't want to admit he was apprehensive —but he was. So much could go wrong.

Brynlee's steps slowed and she pointed to something in the distance. He already knew what it was: a sixteen-foot waterfall that cascaded to a pool below. The attraction was popular with hikers. Any other day, Boone would enjoy the view also.

"Look at that," Brynlee said, her voice full of wonder.

"When this is all over, I'll bring you back here so you can appreciate it. Unfortunately, we don't have that luxury right now."

Brynlee took a few more steps, pulling her gaze away from the sight. "What's it called?"

"Lost Falls."

"Lost Falls. I like that." She continued to walk. "We're going back a different way. I didn't see this earlier."

"This path is a little longer, but we should be able to navigate it faster." He nodded, indicating they should keep moving.

Brynlee kept walking behind him. He pushed branches out of the way as they trekked forward. The air was getting cooler—much cooler. And darkness would be on them before they knew it.

As Boone heard a stick break in the distance, apprehension pinched his spine.

He froze in the middle of the heavily wooded area and put a finger over his lips. Brynlee nearly collided with him. Boone gripped her arm and motioned for her to remain quiet.

Alarm spread through her gaze as she realized that he'd heard something.

Someone was close.

Or something.

Boone studied the landscape around him. The trees. The boulders. The shadows.

Even the birds had gone quiet.

But he saw nothing. No one.

So why did his gut tell him that trouble was near?

He reached for Brynlee's hand. Still motioning for her to be quiet, he began leading her through the woods. They couldn't stay where they were. No, they needed to move—the more quickly, the better.

"What's wrong, Boone?" Brynlee whispered.

"We're being hunted."

The color drained from her face. "What are we going to do?"

"We need to find somewhere that will act as a shelter for us." The challenging part would be finding an area like that here in the middle of the forest.

"I heard a rumor that there's an old house up there, not far from the waterfall," Brynlee whispered. "I saw it on an old map. It had Lost Falls on it."

An old house? Maybe Boone had heard something about an old building in the past. There was so much of this area that was unexplored.

Boone had no idea if Brynlee was right, but, if she was, that would be an answer to prayer for sure.

Still being careful, they continued quietly down the mountainside.

Boone still sensed unseen eyes on them. Adrenaline pounded through his blood. His instincts were tight, poised to react.

He didn't get easily spooked out here in the wild. But right now, every part of him could feel the danger around them.

As they stepped beyond a boulder, he heard a rustle in the undergrowth. He turned toward the sound and saw something emerge from the shadows.

He didn't know what it was.

But he knew one thing. They were in danger.

"Run!" he shouted.

He and Brynlee took off.

34

Brynlee's lungs burned. Her muscles felt tight. Sweat covered her skin.

As a roar sounded behind her, her fear only intensified.

It was the beast. The Skookum. Whatever it was.

He'd found them. And now he would kill them —unless they got away.

As the trail disappeared around them, she prayed harder. Moved faster.

The beast was close. Close enough she could hear its grunts. Feel the branches breaking around it. Feel that death was near.

Breathing down her neck.

They had to find somewhere safe. They had to find it now.

She only hoped her initial assessment was correct.

Was this the area where her family's old house was located? She'd seen that waterfall. She knew her father talked about Lost Falls being close—just to the north. She'd seen that roughly drawn map.

Please be there. Please.

Boone's pace quickened. He pulled harder.

She could still feel the beast. Feel that it was on their heels.

Hear its growls and rapid breaths.

Then she heard a moan.

Brynlee glanced over her shoulder in time to see that the beast had stumbled.

His fall would buy them some time.

Thank goodness.

Boone continued to pull her forward. Brynlee could hardly breathe. Hardly think. She just moved.

As they rounded some trees, a building appeared.

Was this it? The house Brynlee had been looking for?

It didn't matter.

All that mattered right now was that this building offered safety. For a moment, at least.

Boone seemed to spot it at the same time. He pulled harder. Moved more quickly. "We can make it there."

Brynlee didn't dare glance behind her. Didn't want to see how close the creature was. If he'd caught up with them. But she didn't hear it now. Didn't hear his footsteps or branches breaking or heavy breathing.

Maybe they did have a chance.

They reached the old cabin. Boone reached for the door.

It was unlocked.

He shoved her inside and slammed the door. He reached for a lock.

There was nothing.

They kept moving.

Boone kept pulling her. Up the stairs. Into a closet.

He closed the door and sat down, pulling her against him.

They sat so close that Brynlee could feel his heart beating into her back. That she heard his quick intake of air.

"Quiet," he whispered.

They weren't out of danger yet, she realized.

And Brynlee prayed with everything in her that they might stay safe.

Boone pulled Brynlee closer and listened.

He'd like to think they were out of the woods—literally and figuratively—but he wasn't ready to let his guard down.

That creature had been close. Too close.

He waited to hear a telltale sign. There was nothing.

The air around them felt charged with danger, though.

As silence marched around them, he caught a whiff of Brynlee's hair. What was that scent? It reminded him of coconut and flowers. And it was divine.

As Boone held her right now, he knew with certainty that he would do whatever it took to protect her. She'd quickly gained a place in his heart. And no one had done that since Katherine.

He didn't even think it was possible.

Silence passed. Nothing. Had they lost the beast?

"Do you think he's gone?" Brynlee whispered.

She craned her neck until Boone could vaguely make out her face. See her hopeful eyes. Hear her breathless voice.

He wanted to say yes. He wanted to confirm that they were finally safe.

But something internal told him to stay.

He put his finger over his lips again.

He felt the tremble that raked through Brynlee's body as he did.

He wanted more than anything to alleviate her fears. But that would be foolish. It wouldn't help either of them.

A creak sounded nearby.

That had come from inside the house, hadn't it?

Brynlee seemed to hear it also. She froze so quickly that Boone wasn't even sure she was breathing.

Another creak sounded. Then another.

The creature was definitely inside.

And those creaks . . . they sounded close.

Had it come upstairs?

A shadow passed by the slit at the bottom of the door.

As Brynlee gasped, Boone put his hand over her mouth. They could not give away their location. Their lives depended on their silence right now.

35

Brynlee felt like she was suffocating. Like she couldn't breathe.

Death felt close.

Like it lurked right outside the door.

And every creak, every shadow that fell seemed like a nail in her coffin.

Boone pulled her closer, his breathing steady and even beside her.

She closed her eyes, finding a moment of comfort in that fact.

But as another squeak sounded, her nerves ratcheted up again.

That beast was outside the closet. Only wood stood between them.

Would he find them?

And, when he did, what would he do? Boone had lost his gun.

She remembered watching the beast's claws slash into the neck of that hiker. She remembered the blood. Death.

A whimper wanted to escape, but Boone's hand pressed into her mouth again.

Both of them kept deadly still.

More heavy footsteps sounded.

Then paused.

She pressed her eyes closed.

Had the creature discovered she and Boone were there?

Fear clutched her, stabbing at her heart until she wanted to bend with pain.

Then the footsteps quickened.

Hurried.

Went . . . away?

What?

They still didn't dare move. No, it was too risky.

Neither said anything as the minutes ticked by.

Finally, when they'd heard nothing for what seemed like an hour—though she was sure it hadn't been that long—Boone moved his hand away from her mouth and relaxed a little.

Still, neither moved.

That's when Brynlee realized just how tangled she and Boone were. She was snug in his embrace, her back against his chest, his body acting like a shell around her.

And she liked the security she had with Boone. She liked feeling his closeness. Smelling his ruggedly earthy soap. Feeling the bristles of his unshaven face.

In fact, she never felt as invigorated as she did around him. Never. Not around Will. Not around anyone she'd ever dated.

There was something about Boone Wilder that was different.

And Brynlee wasn't sure if she liked that or if it terrified her.

She froze again and held her breath so she could listen.

There was still nothing.

No sounds in the house.

No creaks or shadows.

Where had that beast gone?

Boone leaned back, pulling away from her before whispering, "I need to go check things out."

Brynlee wanted to cling to him. To tell him not to go. Beg him to stay with her.

But she didn't. She knew it would be no use.

Instead, she nodded. "Be careful."

Boone's gaze met hers, sending an unspoken message. He didn't have to say anything. She knew he wouldn't let her down.

"I will be," he finally said. "Stay here."

Carefully, Boone stood. He counted to three before opening the door.

He had no idea what to expect on the other side.

Was the beast waiting them out? Hiding? Anticipating attacking when they were least expecting it?

Or had the creature left, as it sounded like had happened?

Boone scanned the room.

It was dark in here. Wood walls. Ceiling. Floor.

Only small windows.

The creature was nowhere in sight.

Carefully, he stepped out. Closed the door behind him.

He hated to leave Brynlee in there. But he couldn't risk taking her out here either. Not until he assessed the risk.

Slowly, Boone moved toward the stairs, remaining near the wall with his pocketknife in his hand, blade extended.

His heart pounded into his chest, reminding him of his military days. Of special operations. Of going into battle with an unseen enemy. He was honored to have served his country. But that kind of life wasn't for him. No, he was more of a free spirit than what the military had required of him. And this situation right now was bringing all that back.

He reached the stairs. His throat ached with dryness as he took the first step down, uncertain what he'd face when he reached the bottom.

The wood cried out from beneath his feet. He froze for a moment, expecting to see movement. Expecting a jump scare.

Nothing.

Light filtered in through the windows. Instead of finding comfort in the sight, the scene was eerie. How long had it been since anyone was in this place? And how had Brynlee known it was here?

He'd have to ask her that—later.

For now, Boone had to ensure they were going to get out of here safely.

But as he paused near the door, another realization hit him. Whoever had come here had opened the door.

A bear wouldn't have been able to turn this knob.

No, the creature had definitely been a human.

Boone didn't know if that made him feel better or worse. But he knew one thing: they weren't safe, and they wouldn't be until they caught whoever was behind this.

36

Brynlee remained huddled in the closet, her knees pulled to her chest, muttering prayers. At any moment, she expected to hear a roar. A scream. A thud.

Every time she imagined those things playing out, a new round of panic rose in her.

She didn't want anything to happen to Boone. But she also didn't want to be left alone in these woods with that creature.

She held her breath.

Were those footsteps? Coming toward her?

It was Boone, right? Not the creature.

But, until she saw it with her own eyes, she couldn't be sure.

A moment later, the steps stopped near the closet. Her head swam as she waited. Dreaded.

The door flung open.

Brynlee drew back, unsure what to expect.

But Boone stood there.

The air left her lungs.

Boone.

Thank goodness. He extended his hand to help her from the closet. As his fingers closed over hers, Brynlee's heartbeat accelerated a moment. Why did the man keep having that effect on her?

"You're okay," she muttered, quickly scanning him for any sign of injury.

He nodded, his gaze still checking everything around them. "I'm fine. But it's not safe for us to continue back this evening."

Another round of fear seized her at the implications of his words. "So what are we going to do?"

"I think we should hunker down here until morning. The last thing we want is to traverse these trails at night. We'll just be setting ourselves up for failure. And failure means . . ."

"Death," she finished, her throat dry. "But won't we be sitting ducks here?"

"At least we have shelter here. That will go a long way."

"But doesn't that creature know we're here? He followed us . . ."

Boone frowned. "I don't know. We lost him for a few minutes. If he knew we were here, why did he leave? Why didn't he just finish us off when he could?"

"Great question." Brynlee shivered and looked around the dark space. "There are worse places to stay, I suppose."

"Let's see if we can find some blankets. We won't be able to start a fire—it will draw too much attention and let him know we're still here. It's going to get cold, so we'll need to stay warm."

Brynlee nodded and began wandering around the space. They could take some blankets off the beds, but they were going to be dusty. It was obvious no one had been here for years. Though the place was neat and tidy, it was also abandoned and unused.

She opened a trunk and found some quilts. She brought one to her nose. To her surprise, it smelled fairly clean—like mothballs. Maybe the trunk had protected the fabric from the elements.

"I think we can use these," she told Boone.

"Perfect. I think we should set up camp upstairs. Put as much space between the front door and ourselves as possible. I'm going to push some furniture in front of the doors, as well as set a few other traps that will alert us if someone comes in here."

"Sounds like a plan." She began shaking out the quilts, preparing for the coming evening. It was already getting dark outside. Once the sun sank, darkness came quickly.

Brynlee wasn't sure exactly how to set up or where. But as she worked, she paused and looked at some of the quilts. They were beautiful. Intricate. Told such wonderful stories.

Stories that her grandparents wanted to pass on.

Yes, this was the cabin her dad had told her about. She felt certain of it.

Because this mountain had belonged to that side of the family.

A swell of longing rose in her. She wished she could enjoy exploring this space, that she could relish in her family's history. But this wasn't the time.

As she pulled out another blanket, she saw a book tucked there. She picked it up. It almost looked like . . . a journal.

She ran her hand over the leather cover and then opened it, staring at the brittle page below.

Yes, this was a journal. She began scanning the entries. The scrawl made it look like a woman had written the words there. It was dated thirty years ago.

Thirty years?

This would have most likely have belonged to her grandparents then. Grandparents she'd never met.

An entry on one of the last pages caught her eye and she gasped.

There's a creature out in these woods. He's been stalking the cabin. We awoke this morning and found claw marks outside the door. Herb says we can't stay here anymore—not until this creature is caught. But no one believes us. I don't know where we'll go or what we'll do. I hate to leave this mountain . . . but we have no other choice.

Tears pressed into Brynlee's eyes.

That creature . . . he wasn't a figment of Brynlee's imagination. No, he'd stalked these woods for decades.

And now he was stalking Brynlee.

Brynlee stuffed the journal into her backpack as she heard footsteps coming up the stairs.

"I did the best I could to secure this place," Boone said. He placed something on the table. "I found some knives. At least it's some kind of protection if we need it."

"And I found these old quilts. They should keep us warm."

"Perfect." He walked over to the little nest she'd set up. After grabbing his backpack, he lowered himself on the floor and pulled up a blanket. "It's already getting cold, isn't it?"

She shivered at his words. She'd been thinking the same thing. "It is."

He patted the space beside him. With a touch of nerves, she lowered herself there. He shared his blanket with her. They both leaned back against the wall for a moment, neither saying anything.

"How did you say you knew this place was here?" Boone turned toward her.

Brynlee shrugged, trying to figure out how to respond. "I did research on this area before I came. That included looking at some old maps."

"It's just that I've been up this mountain many times. I've never seen this before."

"Well, I am an interior designer. I have an eye for detail . . . sometimes." Guilt beat at her.

Tell him, an internal voice urged.

But the words wouldn't leave Brynlee's mouth. She knew how things would change once Boone knew the whole truth. She wasn't sure she was ready to face that yet.

Thankfully, he didn't press anymore. Instead, he grabbed his backpack and began scrounging through it. "Either way, it's a good thing we found this."

"I agree."

He reached inside his bag, grabbed something, and handed it to her. "For you."

Brynlee stared at the muffin he pulled out of a plastic container.

"What's this?" she asked. "Did you bake this morning before we left?"

He shrugged. "What's the big deal? It's a muffin . . ."

"I see that, but . . ."

He raised his eyebrows and held it up like a prize. "It's vegetarian. And it's blueberry."

Her throat tightened. "Blueberry?"

He shrugged again. "Yeah, I noticed you like blueberry so I decided to get this kind. I know the woman who owns the bakery in town, so I wanted to grab something for the trip there. I thought this was perfect." He did a double take at her. "Am I wrong?"

Tears pressed at her eyes—tears that she wanted to go away. "No, this looks great. Thank you."

"If this is great then why do you look like you're going to cry?" Boone broke off a piece of his own muffin and put it in his mouth.

Brynlee let out an airy laugh, realizing how silly she must look. "I'm sorry. It's just that . . . well, I don't know. It sounds crazy, but it just touched me that you even noticed that."

"I'm glad I did something right." He handed her the muffin.

"You've done a lot right." Brynlee swallowed hard as she said the words, knowing how they might sound.

Boone's gaze caught hers. He reached up and ran a finger across her cheek. "I think that was a compliment."

Her throat felt so dry she could hardly swallow. Why was Boone having this effect on her? It didn't make any sense.

But as his fingers lingered near her neck, her heart rate continued to ratchet up.

She wanted to reach up and feel the hair on his cheeks. Run her fingers through the curls at his neck. To explore the lines on his face.

This was trouble. Big trouble.

"I want to kiss you right now," he murmured.

"You know, if you have to announce it, it usually spoils the moment a bit." She smiled teasingly.

Boone didn't smile back. His intense gaze locked on hers. His fingers still trailed her hair, her neck. "You don't understand."

"Then explain it to me." She really just wanted him to kiss her.

"I haven't wanted to kiss anyone since . . ."

Brynlee's breath caught. She knew exactly what Boone was saying, even though he didn't finish his sentence.

Since Katherine.

Warmth flooded her heart.

The next thing she knew, his lips covered hers. Tugging. Curious. Almost tentative.

But only for a minute.

She wrapped her arms around his neck as heat surged through her. Her fingers reached up. Touched the hair at the nape of his neck. Explored the tousled curls.

Finally, they both pulled back—though barely. They remained close enough that they could easily do that again.

Which wasn't a bad idea.

"I can't even apologize for that," Boone murmured.

"Me neither."

"But I don't know what this means . . ."

"The good news is that I don't think we have to figure it out right now."

A smile spread across his face, and Boone pulled her toward him until Brynlee's head hit his chest. His arms tightened around her.

To her surprise, she felt herself relaxing in his embrace. Relishing the sound of his heartbeat against her ear. Eating up the warmth he offered.

Romance was the last thing Brynlee had expected to find when she came here. Yet, maybe it was just what she wanted—and needed.

37

Boone felt the steady rise and fall of Brynlee's breaths as she leaned against his chest. They were still in the corner with quilts over them. His arms were around her as they rested against the wall.

Holding her felt good . . . it felt right.

But he'd never expected this. Never expected his feelings to develop so fast. So hard.

Brynlee had captured a place in his heart that he thought was permanently closed.

He leaned into her now, smelling the sweet scent of her shampoo.

Now that he held her in his arms, he never wanted to let her go.

Despite those thoughts, his mind drifted to Katherine. To the marks on that tree.

Was he reading too much into this?

No, he knew he wasn't. The only way that tally mark should be on that tree was if Katherine had left it.

What if someone else had left it?

But no one else knew that little space was there. The carvings were near the base of the tree, toward the back. No one else would think to look there unless they knew the marks were there.

But he needed a moment to explore the idea of an alternate scenario that had played out that day with Kat. Everyone thought her line had broken. A few people speculated that he'd tampered with it.

The truth, as he'd known it, was that Kat had tried to climb to the top and beat Boone there. Her line had broken, sending her falling to her death. Boone had found her after he'd crossed the Razor Back and arrived at Dead Man's Bluff, feeling triumphant.

Then surprised.

He'd looked over the ledge, expecting to see Kat climbing up.

Instead, he'd seen her dead body at the bottom.

His lungs tightened at the memories.

But now a new theory wanted to form. A theory where she'd reached the top. Marked her arrival. Waited for him.

But what if someone else was already there, waiting for her to arrive?

Still, how could that result in something malicious?

If his theory was true, someone would have seen Kat there. Cut her line. And then shoved her off the cliff.

Boone's stomach clenched at the thought. He could hardly handle thinking about it.

Yet the thought also caused anger to surge through him.

He'd already thought her death was senseless. But if it was on purpose . . .

But why? Why would someone want Kat dead? Had she seen something when she got to the top? Had someone targeted her? She was a physical trainer. She didn't have any enemies that Boone could think of.

So it just didn't make sense.

But he was more determined than ever to find some answers.

As the thoughts continued to pummel him, a noise downstairs caught his ear.

What was that? it almost sounded like . . .

He jerked upright.

He'd set up some cans on the windowsill. If anyone tried to open one of those windows, the cans would fall to the floor, alerting him to someone's presence.

He waited another moment.

And then he clearly heard a clank as something hit the ground.

Brynlee jerked awake as she felt movement around her. She opened her sleepy eyes—she'd been sleeping deeply—and spotted Boone beside her.

Her cheeks warmed.

Boone. That was right. But before she could revel in their kiss, she saw the alarm on his face. He stuck something in her hand.

She glanced down.

A knife.

Her blissful moment turned into panic.

"I heard something downstairs. I need to check it out. Get into the closet and stay there until I tell you to come out. Okay?"

No . . . this nightmare just kept continuing. When would it end?

She didn't have time to argue or whine. Boone ushered her back into the closet, butcher knife in hand. He gave her one last look—a look full of concern—before shutting the door.

Her heart pounded in her chest. Now Boone was

out there again with that thing. What if he wasn't as lucky this time? What if the beast confronted him? If there was a fight?

All Boone had was a knife. It would be no match against that creature's claws.

She remembered the journal entry she'd read. Remembered the fact that her grandparents had also encountered this creature. That put all of this into a totally different light.

What if this was a Skookum? Brynlee didn't normally believe in things like this, but she couldn't deny the facts in front of her.

It seemed like the incidents with him were mostly confined to this mountain. Why was that? Was this mountain his home?

When she had a chance, she'd look through the journal more. Maybe there were answers there.

And she had other big choices to make. Did she fulfill her father's wishes of trying to open a resort on Dead Man's Bluff so others could enjoy this area? Or did she honor Boone by leaving this place with the natural beauty it had?

The choices clashed inside her.

She paused and listened again.

What was happening with Boone down there? Did he see anything? Was that creature hiding, just waiting to take Boone by surprise?

She gripped the knife in her hand.

How could she just stay in here while Boone was out there protecting her with his life?

She stood, even though her legs wobbled.

She stared at the door a moment, willing herself to open it. To be brave.

Or stupid.

There was a fine line sometimes.

She licked her lips, determined not to be a wimp.

But before she could open the door, she heard footsteps again.

Someone was outside the closet door.

Was it Boone or the beast?

38

Boone jerked open the door and saw Brynlee standing there, knife raised.

As soon as she saw him, the knife clattered from her hands and onto the floor.

She looked terrified.

Without a second thought, he pulled her into his arms and held her. "It's okay."

"I thought . . ."

"I know. Some of the cans fell over near a window. But I think the window was drafty and a breeze came through. Everything is okay."

She leaned into him. "I'm so glad. I thought . . ."

"I know. It's okay, though."

He held her another moment. He could feel her heart racing against his chest. Feel the quiver of her limbs.

This situation would terrify anyone.

"I just want to get off this mountain," she murmured into his chest.

He felt the same way. But it was only 3:30 a.m. They needed to wait until the sun started to rise before they set out. "We're going to get through this."

They'd leave at the first chance. He'd continue trying to call Luke.

By now, certainly Luke was aware that something was wrong. Luke and Abe both had been expecting Boone to return this evening. But they'd be too discerning to send a search party out in the middle of the night.

They had no choice but to wait this out until then.

He had a feeling neither he nor Brynlee would be getting much more rest tonight.

Brynlee leaned against Boone and tried to forget her worries. Dwelling on them right now would do no good anyway. They were doing everything they could to protect themselves. Staying here was the only option until daybreak.

"So, you like being an interior designer?" Boone asked.

They were both situated on the quilts again,

trying to stay warm. They may have exchanged a few more kisses as they'd passed the time, each one sending tingles through her. But now they talked and, on occasion, popped some boiled peanuts into their mouths.

"I do like it. There's just something about making a place feel warm and welcoming that makes me feel good."

"So what would you do with my store, if you could change something?"

Brynlee shrugged. "I'm not sure I'd change anything."

"What? I decorated that place myself."

She smiled. "And it shows your personality. I think its rustic and outdoorsy. That's exactly what people want who come into your store. It's authentic, and people like that."

"Good to know I've got some skills."

She pulled her feet beneath her. "I'm sorry to hear about your financial struggles there. I know it's a lot of money you need to come up with."

"Tell me about it."

"So what are you going to do?"

"I have no idea. I keep hoping a solution will drop in my lap."

"As my dad said, luck isn't a plan."

Boone let out an airy chuckle. "No, it's not. Then I'm looking for a divine gift from God."

"Well, I hope you get it." As she said the words, an idea began to form in her mind.

Maybe she'd been looking at things from the wrong perspective this whole time. What if . . . ?

She pressed her lips together. She couldn't speak anything out loud right now, but her thoughts raced.

She had a solution. For her. For Boone.

But she had to check with the county about it.

Excitement pulsed through her.

"Now that you've spread your dad's ashes, I guess you'll be headed back to Pennsylvania?"

Boone's words caused her heart to thump inside her throat.

That was right. She had a life waiting for her back home.

It wasn't the most fulfilling life. She loved her job, and she had a few friends. But her mom was gone and so was her dad. Though she'd met up with her father's family, they weren't like her. They were affluent and everything had been handed to them.

Now that she'd been here in Fog lake . . . she hated to think about leaving.

That thought was crazy, though. How could one place change her perspective so quickly?

Or was it Boone who had changed her mind?

Still, she needed to be careful. He hadn't promised her anything. Nor would he. It was too soon. They were just starting to get to know each other. And even though their chemistry felt crazy, there was more to a relationship than that.

"Brynlee?" Boone said.

She remembered his question. *I guess you'll head back to Pennsylvania now . . .*

"That was the plan."

"Was?"

She shrugged. "Is? I mean, you're right. I came here to do what I needed."

He licked his lips and nodded slowly. "Of course."

She wanted to say that she could be swayed. But the time wasn't right. They didn't know each other well enough for her to say that. To do that.

Still, she couldn't deny the heaviness she felt at the thought.

Boone pulled her toward him and wrapped his arms around her.

She'd never felt so safe, even with the craziness going on around them.

And that was a feeling she didn't want to give up. But she knew she shouldn't hold on too tightly to anything around her. Because everyone around her had always looked out for themselves and never her. How could she trust that this feeling would last?

She couldn't. She'd be wise to keep that in mind.

"Did you see that trunk over there?" Boone murmured.

"What?"

"Look under the bed. It looks like a trunk there."

Brynlee's breath caught. "It sure does."

"Let's see what's inside." He stood and walked across the floor. She immediately missed his warmth but didn't argue. Some space between them would be good right now.

Boone opened the truck and let out a grunt. A moment later, he held something up.

It was a bear skin.

No, it wasn't a bear skin. It was a costume.

She glanced down and saw claws. A mask.

The two of them exchanged a look.

This confirmed what Brynlee had suspected all along. This wasn't a bear. It wasn't a Skookum. This was a person who was disguising himself in order to kill others.

39

Bright and early the next morning, Brynlee and Boone started back toward the trailhead with the bear costume crammed into Boone's backpack, ready to be turned in as evidence.

As soon as Brynlee stepped out from the cabin, she braced herself for something to reach out and grab her. To finish what he started.

But there was nothing. Only birds singing. The wind rustling leaves. And a beautiful landscape.

In other circumstances, this would seem idyllic. Like a perfect moment with nature.

But Brynlee knew the danger that lurked beyond all this beauty.

Boone reached back, offering his hand as they continued through the forest. Warmth rushed through her.

She took his hand into hers, relishing the feel of it between her fingers. This time, he hadn't offered it out of pure helpfulness. This time, it was because of the bond they'd formed.

Her cheeks flushed at the thought. Flushed as she remembered their time together. As she remembered how tender Boone could be.

"We need to remain aware of everything around us," Boone said as he helped her over some rocks. "As soon as I get reception, I'll call for help. Until then, we need to keep our eyes open for potential danger."

Another shiver rushed down Brynlee's spine. "Sounds good."

"And even though luck isn't a plan, we're going to need a good measure of luck right now also—and a whole lot of faith."

"I think I like faith better than I do luck." She glanced up at him, feeling the amusement dancing in her gaze.

Boone glanced back and smiled. "Me too, usually. But I'm already feeling pretty lucky since I met you."

He paused long enough to plant a quick kiss on her lips.

Pure pleasure warmed Brynlee's veins. She longed for this thing developing between her and Boone to be more than just a flash-in-the-pan relationship. She could see herself being with someone like Boone . . . forever.

The thought made her throat go dry.

What was she going to do? Sooner or later Boone was going to find out her ulterior motives for being here. Even though Brynlee had a new plan, the Planning Council would still need to approve it.

And based on her previous conversations with Boone, there was no way he would be on board. No, he'd be the biggest opponent, for that matter.

The realization clashed inside Brynlee, causing her stomach to knot.

Just tell him.

Yet she couldn't bring the words to leave her mouth. She didn't want things to change. Yet she'd dug this hole for herself. Now she had to figure a way out.

A few steps later, Boone's phone rang. They had reception!

Boone exchanged a glance with Brynlee before putting the phone to his ear. "Luke. I've never been so glad to hear from you."

He muttered a few more things and gave Luke his location. A team was coming to meet them now. They weren't far away, from what Brynlee could gather. Maybe twenty minutes, max.

She prayed they could make it that far without any surprises. Their hike so far today had been quiet and peaceful. Was that just a façade for the danger lurking around them?

Boone's muscles seemed to tense at whatever Luke was telling him.

Brynlee braced herself for more bad news. More facts about this madman terrorizing the town . . . terrorizing her.

As Luke ended his call, he turned toward Brynlee, a new look in his eyes. Was that accusation? Her muscles tightened.

"Brynlee, do you know a man named Stephen Royce?"

She sucked in a deep breath at hearing his name. "Why? Did something happen?"

"That's the name of the man who was found dead yesterday morning. Your card was in his pocket."

Boone continued to process what Luke had just told him. He stared at Brynlee, watching her expression. Why did she look so regretful right now? What wasn't she telling him?

The answers were on the edge of his reason, but maybe he didn't want to face the truth.

"I can explain, Boone . . ."

So there *was* more to her story. He should have

known. This had never just been just about spreading her father's ashes. There was another reason she was interested in Dead Man's Bluff.

The truth slammed into his mind.

"You're the one who wants to develop the area, aren't you?" The words left a sour taste in his mouth. He desperately wanted her to deny them, to tell him he was wrong. Her dad was a businessman who liked this area . . . he was the owner of Brinkley and Sons, wasn't he?

"It's not like you think it is." Her voice came out rushed, frantic.

"Then what is it like?" He let go of her hand and stepped back.

She frowned and pushed her hair behind her ear. "Developing this mountain was my dad's idea. This is my family's land."

"Your dad was Tom Brinkley . . ."

Her gaze pleaded with him to understand. "That's right. Like I said, I only got to know him in the year or so before he died."

"That's how you knew to find that cabin, isn't it?" He let out a puff of air, feeling stupid. More than stupid. Feeling used.

"He did tell me about the old family cabin," Brynlee said. "That it wasn't far from the waterfall. I'd never been there before. But he did tell me that the deed to the land had been left there. I knew I'd eventually need to find it."

Boone's mind continued to race. "Your dad tried to develop this mountain ten years ago or so but was unsuccessful."

"He told me. He told me about the opposition. Told me what to expect."

"But you wanted to do it anyway?" He should have seen the writing on the wall. How could he have been so stupid? Was any of this real? He was beginning to doubt it.

"It's more complicated than that. My dad really did want me to spread his ashes here. But he also told me about this crazy dream he had to share this area with others."

Boone started back down the path, his back rigid with tension. "Developing it isn't the way to do it."

"I realize that." Brynlee scrambled behind him. "I actually have another idea—"

"Save it."

"But, Boone, please. Listen to me."

He shook his head. "I don't want to hear it, Brynlee. You've been dishonest with me from the moment we met. I suppose the moments we shared together weren't anything but a show either, were they?" He glanced over his shoulder, throwing a scowl at her.

"That's not true. All of that was real. I wanted to tell you, Boone—"

He stopped and turned toward her again. "Then why didn't you?"

Brynlee nibbled on her bottom lip a moment, her eyes filling with moisture. "Because I was afraid of this."

"You had good reason to be."

"Come on, Boone. You and I both know that you wouldn't have given me the time of day if you'd known who I really was."

"You're right. I wouldn't have. But I don't want anyone here throwing around their money and destroying this area so they can make a few more bucks."

"It's not like that." She crossed her arms.

He stared at her another moment. She looked so beautiful. Yet she was deceitful. She was trouble. Boone should have listened to his gut reaction about her. "So you hired that surveyor, didn't you?"

She pressed her eyes closed and her voice sounded somber as she said, "I did. I had to in order to continue."

"He's dead."

She blanched at his words. "I told him not to go into these woods. I told him to use a drone. That it wasn't safe. He must not have listened. Boone, I just wish you'd hear me out—"

"There's nothing more to hear. I'm done with this. I'm done acting as security for you. You can keep your money. I don't want it." Boone sliced his hand through the air.

"But—"

"There's nothing you can say that will change my mind." He turned and continued walking.

Brynlee started to speak again, but before she could try and convince him, voices sounded in the distance.

The rescue team had arrived.

Perfect. Brynlee would be out of his hands.

Now Boone could devote all his energy into fighting for this mountain and this town . . . and getting Brynlee Parker out of his system.

40

The next few hours were a blur for Brynlee.

She and Boone had been rescued. Gone back down to the trailhead. The sheriff had driven her to the station, where she'd given a statement about Stephen Royce.

Even Luke was acting colder now that he'd realized the truth. Still professional but definitely frosty.

Boone wouldn't even look at her.

Everyone in town was going to hate Brynlee now.

She knew she had no more reason to stay here in Fog Lake. She'd come here and found a life she didn't even know she wanted. And just as Brynlee had realized that, she also realized that people here would never accept her.

Never.

Luke told her she was free to leave town. He'd also made a point of letting her know that Harper was at the house if she wanted to pick up her things. Deputy Cruise drove her there.

As they pulled away from the station, Brynlee glanced back in time to see Boone step outside. His eyes met hers, but instead of the warmth and acceptance she craved, he glared at her. She was clearly the enemy now.

If only he'd given her a chance to explain.

Then again, Brynlee should have been the one to tell him the truth.

In that regard, she couldn't even blame Boone for his anger. She'd brought this on herself. She'd just never expected to develop these kinds of feelings or connections so fast. So deeply. So strongly.

And now it was all ruined. She had no one to blame but herself.

Deputy Cruise dropped her off at Luke and Harper's. Brynlee's feet felt like they had lead weights attached as she walked up the front steps. Before she could even knock, Harper opened the door.

Brynlee halfway expected Harper to leave her stuff on the porch. Instead, she ushered her inside, a subdued look on her face.

"I'm just going to get my things." Brynlee pointed to the hallway where her room was.

Harper nodded, her actions clearly showing her disappointment.

Brynlee grabbed her bag, took one last glance around the space that had felt so homey only a day before, and then stepped back toward Harper.

She frowned at her hostess, wondering exactly what she should say. There was nothing that would make things better. She knew that without a doubt.

Brynlee settled for, "I'm really sorry. But thank you for your hospitality."

Brynlee stepped outside, not waiting for Harper to force a response. There was nothing to say.

"Wait," Harper said.

Brynlee paused on the porch and looked back at her. "Yes?"

"Look, I know everyone in town is mad at you. No one here wants to see that mountain developed. This land is precious to the town."

"I understand that," Brynlee said. "I never wanted to upset people. Of course, when I came here, I didn't understand how these mountains were the heartbeat of this town. And now that I know . . . well, I feel differently."

"What do you mean?" Harper tilted her head, no judgment in her tone.

"I mean that I came here with the idea to build a resort on that mountaintop, just like my dad had wanted. But when I finally visited Dead Man's Bluff,

I had a different idea." Brynlee shared her new plan with her.

Harper nodded as she listened. She remained silent a moment before saying, "I actually like that."

Her words brought a temporary relief. But the truth still remained. "But it doesn't matter now. It's too late. Everyone hates me."

"Hate is a strong word." Harper's voice sounded gentle. "We just wish you'd told us why you were really here."

"If I had, none of you would have befriended me. So, I guess I just had to pick my poison. For a few minutes, I really felt like I fit in. Like I'd found a home. That's really all I've ever wanted." Brynlee let out a self-conscious laugh. She hadn't intended on sharing all of that. "But it doesn't matter anymore."

"For what it's worth, I've never seen Boone look at a woman like he looks at you. I just assumed he'd be a bachelor for the rest of his life."

Brynlee wanted to delight in her words. But it didn't matter anymore. She'd blown it. "It's too late."

"Give him time."

Brynlee tried to smile but couldn't. These few days here had changed her in ways she hadn't expected. She was no longer sure what her future would look like. "I think that ship has sailed. Anyway, thanks again for everything, Harper. Maybe now that I'm gone, whoever is behind these attacks will disappear again. I'm sorry for the trouble I brought."

And with those words, she went to her car. It was time to get out of town.

She just had one thing to do first.

Boone could still feel the anger bubbling inside him. He couldn't believe the nerve Brynlee had.

Couldn't believe he'd fallen for her act.

Couldn't believe that beneath her sweet exterior, she'd been a money-hungry developer.

When Boone had told himself he was better off alone, he'd been right. He should have stuck to his guns. If he had, he would have saved himself a lot of heartache.

He shoved the drawer to his cash register shut with a little more force than necessary. He hadn't had anything better to do, so he'd come into work.

"Boss, you okay?" Chigger stared at him from a distance, as if he knew not to get too close.

Boone crossed his arms, unable to shake his mood. "I'm fine."

"I know this is a bad time to bring this up, but Todd stopped by again yesterday while you were gone. Reminded us that we were running out of time."

Boone scowled. "I might as well just close down this store. There's no way I'm going to have the money to make the improvements he says I need."

Chigger stared at him. "Really? That doesn't even sound like you."

"Sometimes I just get tired of fighting, Chigger. It seems a needless battle when decisions have already been made."

"You talking about the store or something else?"

Boone scowled again. "The store, of course."

Chigger raised his hands in surrender.

"Okay, okay. Just asking." Silence stretched for a moment before Chigger continued. "So . . . is it true that thing chased you last night?"

Boone jerked his head toward his employee. "How did you hear that?"

"You know the way people here in town like to talk." Chigger shrugged, like it wasn't a big deal.

"Who exactly talked to you?"

"I went into the diner this morning for breakfast, and people were buzzing about it. A whole bunch of people were there."

"Was Todd one of them?"

"Todd was there. So was Lonny. Abe. I don't know. What does it matter?"

"It matters because no one knew about it until

this morning around eight o'clock. I told Luke." How had word leaked? What if the person responsible had spread the story? His spine went rigid.

Chigger grunted. "Good point. Are you saying . . .?"

"I'm asking, do you remember who started that conversation? It's important, Chigger."

He thought about it a moment before shrugging again. "Nah, man. I came in during the middle of it. You'll have to ask someone else."

"Yeah, I think I'll do that." In fact, maybe he'd do that now. He grabbed his phone, knowing he had no time to waste.

"Oh, one more thing," Chigger continued. "Guess who else came in here yesterday?"

"Who?" Boone hoped this was relevant because he was anxious to find answers.

"A man named Mason Brinkley."

Boone froze as he heard the name. Was that . . . Brynlee's half-brother? "What did he want?"

"He was asking about Dead Man's Bluff. Said his father had wanted to develop it. Said it would be a shame to see it destroyed, that this area was too beautiful to see that happen."

"Wait—did he make it sound like he'd been here before?" He tried to make sense of the man's appearance.

Chigger shrugged. "Yeah, I guess, man. In fact, I think I've seen him here in town before."

But the bad feeling continued to brew in Boone's gut. This was far from over, and Brynlee was still in danger.

---

ow was the time. Brynlee couldn't leave. He wasn't finished with her yet.

He would have gotten her last night. But he had to get back into town. He couldn't risk being out too late. People would have noticed. Asked questions.

It had been Brynlee's lucky evening, but he wanted nothing more than to finish her.

The same this morning.

He would have been out there. At the cabin. Waiting.

But it would have been too obvious. He had a life here in town. He had to keep his identity secret— even though he'd slipped up at breakfast. What had happened wasn't public yet. It wasn't like him to make a mistake like that. But he had to keep the rumors eating away at the town.

Yet the hunger kept growing.

He knew he didn't have much time before he had to act.

He had to find the right opportunity. He had to find Brynlee before she left.

His ancestors were counting on him.

Just like her family had been counting on her.

Unfortunately, she was going to disappoint them.

But would anyone really mourn her when she died?

He didn't think so.

A smile spread across his face at the thought.

It was time to end this.

He couldn't wait any longer.

42

Brynlee had to do one more thing before she headed out of town. Any other business she had to do here could be handled via phone, text, fax, or email.

She wanted to get out of town as quickly as she could.

She wasn't sure if she was imagining it or not, but she felt like everyone she passed gave her dirty looks as she drove through town. Had word really spread that quickly?

She wasn't sure about small-town dynamics, but she imagined that could be the case.

Brynlee found a parking space in the downtown area, climbed out, and headed down the sidewalk. She gripped her purse, praying this would go well.

What she really wanted was to see Boone herself. To talk to him. To explain.

In a perfect world, he'd listen and understand and forgive.

But this world was hardly perfect. She'd learned that at a young age.

"You . . ." someone said beside her.

She turned and saw Witherford Johnson standing there.

She started to keep walking, but she changed her mind and paused instead. She could face whatever was coming to her. *Shame was something you didn't forgive yourself for and you wore it like ashes on your face.* Those were the lyrics to one of her mom's songs.

"I'm surprised you're still showing your face around here." His nostrils flared. "I had no idea you were behind the permit."

"It's actually my father's company who would be financing it. I was just acting as a contact person and project manager."

"And here I thought you were an interior design-er," he scoffed.

She shrugged. "I am."

"You're never going to win this. We've already formed protests and found loopholes."

"I would like to revise my application."

He raised a wiry eyebrow. "I don't know what that means. But you're going to have to come down to the office again and fill out paperwork. Lots of paperwork."

"I will. Just give me some time."

Before he could say anything else, Brynlee kept walking until she reached Abe's Outfitters. Abe looked up from cleaning some kayaks and did what everyone else in town was doing —scowled.

"What are you doing here?" He averted his gaze back to the kayaks and continued to spray water.

The overspray dampened her jeans, but Brynlee ignored it.

"I'd like for you to give this to Boone." She held out her hand.

Abe lowered the hose and stared at the paper there. "What's that?"

"It's a check."

"For what?"

"It's the amount I owe Boone for helping me out."

His gaze darkened again. "I doubt he wants your money."

"But I want him to have it. He needs it for his store."

Abe still said nothing, only stared at her.

"Please," Brynlee said.

Finally, he took it and jammed the check into his back pocket. "I'll see what he says."

"Thank you." She turned to walk away, job done, when Abe called to her.

"You know you'll never be welcome in this town, don't you?"

His words stung like a smack in the face. But she wasn't surprised. Then again, she didn't know what it was like to lay down roots.

She nodded slowly. "Yeah, I know."

She walked back to her SUV, climbed inside, and tried to crank the engine. Nothing happened.

She closed her eyes and leaned against the seat for a minute.

What now? Her car? Would anyone here even fix it for her? Or was she already that hated?

As the thought fluttered through her mind, she glanced over and saw there was a garage within walking distance.

Brynlee was about to find out just how welcome —or unwelcome—she was here in this town.

She walked through the doorway but saw an empty lobby area. "Hello?"

Nothing.

Maybe everyone was in the garage area. Brynlee stepped through the door, expecting to see a repair bay. Instead, she found a hallway with an office in the back.

"Hello?" she called again.

Still nothing.

With a sigh, she pushed open the door across from her.

She paused inside the repair bay. It was empty. And dark. And smelled like motor oil.

This place was closed, wasn't it?

She was going to have to come up with a Plan B and find another mechanic. Otherwise, she'd be spending the night in her broken-down vehicle until she could have it repaired.

She was a survivor. She could do that if she had to. She'd learned through the school of hard knocks, and those lessons were now going to pay off.

As Brynlee turned to step out, she heard a footstep behind her.

She turned to see who it was.

Before she saw anything, a terrible pain spread through her head.

Someone had hit her.

Before she could defend herself or run, everything went black.

As Boone walked toward his truck, he set aside his anger toward Brynlee and dialed her number.

The call went straight to voicemail.

His jaw clenched. He needed to get in touch with her. She could still be in danger. He'd lost Kat, and, to this day, he wished he'd done more to protect her. It was too late for that.

But it wasn't too late for Brynlee.

Where did he even start looking for her?

As his phone rang, he glanced at it. Was Brynlee calling him back?

His heart sank. No such luck. It was Abe.

"What's up?" Boone answered, cranking his truck engine.

"Can you come down to the store? There's something I think you're going to want to see."

"I'll be right there." Maybe Boone would look for Brynlee on the way.

He called Harper as he drove, and she told him that Brynlee had picked up her things.

"She looked really sorry, Boone," Harper said.

"Being sorry doesn't change things."

"No, but forgiveness does."

His jaw clenched. Harper was right, but he wasn't ready to deal with that yet. One thing at a time. His first priority was finding Brynlee.

Fifteen minutes later, Boone pulled to a stop near Abe's Outfitters. His friend was working inside the kiosk. He reached below the counter and pulled something out.

"Brynlee wanted me to give this to you." Abe handed him something.

Boone glanced at the paper. It was a check—for the amount Brynlee had promised to pay him.

He let out a puff of air. She was still stubborn, even after their fight. He'd told her he didn't want this money.

"When did she drop this off?" Boone asked.

Abe shrugged. "Probably twenty minutes ago."

"Did she say if she was leaving?"

"That was my impression. But her SUV is still sitting there."

"Which direction did she walk?"

Abe nodded down the street. "That way, I think."

"Thanks." Boone took off down the road. His gaze scanned the area for Brynlee.

He didn't see her.

Finally, he stopped by her SUV. The black SUV with the claw marks going down the side. His stomach tightened at the sight, which reminded him of just how crazy this person they were dealing with was.

But Brynlee was nowhere to be seen.

He glanced around, hoping to catch a glimpse of her.

"You looking for your friend?" Lonny Thompson paused near him. He held some bags in his hands from the local hardware store. It appeared he'd been out doing errands.

Boone's gaze narrowed. "I am. Have you seen her?"

"I did. She tried to start her SUV but couldn't. The engine wouldn't turn over."

"Did you see where she went?"

He nodded toward a building in the distance. "Saw her head to the garage."

"To Edward's? It's not open today."

Lonny shifted his bags, as if they were getting heavy. "Just telling you what I saw."

Boone started to step that way but paused. "Lonny, what happened to your arm?"

The man's cheeks turned red, and he touched the spot where his cut was. "Nothing. Why?"

"How'd you get that injury?" Was this a clue he needed in order to find Brynlee?

Lonny tugged at his sleeve again. "Long story."

"Give me the short version." Boone's voice left little room for argument.

"I decided to go look in the woods myself." Lonny frowned, as if he were embarrassed. "This whole case has fascinated me. Then again, I've always been fascinated with wildlife. But, as I was hiking, I fell and cut myself. I'm not as young as I once was. I just don't want people to know it."

Boone studied his face. The man appeared to be

telling the truth. But, at this point, Boone wasn't ruling anyone out as a suspect.

"If you hear anything, let me know," Boone said.

Wasting no more time, he took off toward Edward's. He needed to find Brynlee.

Now.

43

Brynlee jerked her eyes open. Her gaze scampered around. She pulled in short, anxious breaths.

Where was she?

Her surroundings slammed into focus.

She was in the cabin. The one where they'd found the bear suit. The one her dad's family owned.

Her legs and arms had scrapes. Her body ached. Her head throbbed.

Had someone carried her up here? Maybe half dragged her through the wilderness?

It was the only thing that made sense. People couldn't drive to this place.

She needed to go.

But when she tried to move, she realized she couldn't. Her hands were tied behind her. To a . . .

post. She was in one of the bedrooms. It was dark. Dusty. Cold.

It felt like a waiting room . . . before death.

She shivered. Not only from the cold but from the situation.

What was this person planning to do with her when he came back? Would he kill her like he killed those hikers? Why hadn't he killed her already?

The bigger question hit her. Who was behind this?

Was it Lonny? The man had that cut on his arm that he'd acted strangely about.

Witherford had strong feelings about this area not being developed.

What if it wasn't someone from this town, at all? What if trouble had followed her here?

Because she could think of someone who would want her dead and who'd have the perfect motive.

Her brother.

She didn't want to think that was true. But she needed to consider all her options. Could Mason have staged all of this in a quest to get her dad's money?

He wouldn't do that . . . would he?

Then again, his motive was the strongest.

Brynlee had no idea what the truth was. But whoever was behind this would be back soon and finish it.

She tugged at the ropes that pinned her arms behind her. At the ones that forced her legs together.

She could scream, but no one would hear her out here. She was all alone.

Just like she'd always been.

Would anyone even look for her?

A cry caught in her throat. She knew the answer.

No.

Boone was the only one who might have, but now he wasn't even speaking to her.

The rest of the town . . . they'd be happy she was gone.

She was going to have to figure out this nightmare on her own. She'd figured out her childhood. Figured out how to fend for herself. She could do it now also.

Maybe her whole life had been preparing her for this moment.

Boone knelt on the ground inside the garage.

Blood. There were subtle drops of blood in the repair bay.

Had Brynlee come in here? Had someone attacked her?

The bad feeling continued to grow in his gut. He

should have never left her alone—even after he found out the truth.

Think, Boone. Think.

Okay, if someone had grabbed her, this person could have stuffed Brynlee into his car and taken her somewhere.

But where? Where would someone take Brynlee?

There was only one place that came to mind.

Dead Man's Bluff. That's what all of this was about, wasn't it?

That's where Boone needed to go. But he needed to assemble a team first. That mountain was too big to traverse alone. He needed backup. And he needed more eyes on the area.

He called Luke and told him what was going on.

Now he needed to figure out who was behind this.

Mason Brinkley?

Who else could it be? Big Ben was still behind bars.

Todd Michaels?

Boone couldn't see him doing this.

But it was someone who felt protective of Dead Man's Bluff. Someone who wouldn't let anything stop him.

And if Boone didn't find Brynlee in time, she was going to die. He had no doubt about that. That mountain couldn't claim another life.

44

The minutes ticked past. Brynlee hadn't been able to loosen her bindings. That left her nothing else to do but sit here and wait for whoever had left her to return.

Tears pressed into her eyes. She couldn't give up this easily. But what else could she do?

She needed to figure out who was behind this. If she knew that, maybe she could strategize a way to convince him this was a bad idea. It was a long shot . . . but she was desperate.

She continually reviewed the suspects. Who was she missing?

Whoever it was had been large.

She could probably rule out Lonny. The man was older, frailer. She couldn't see him hauling her up here.

What about Mason? It seemed ludicrous he would go through such measures. However, he could afford to hire someone. But why? Did he think he'd get more money if he was able to develop this land himself?

The man had never liked her, and he'd seemed ruthless.

She was never going to find acceptance with that side of her family. She wished she'd realized that sooner. Maybe she wouldn't have gone on this crazy quest.

Had she come to fulfill her father's wishes? Or was she trying to impress her half-brothers?

She wasn't sure. It could be a little of both.

Either way, she'd always done life on her own. She needed to accept that outcome for the future as well.

Focus, Brynlee. Focus.

Who else could be behind this? She needed to think everything through.

She tugged at the ropes around her wrists and ankles again. It was no use. They were tied tight. She wasn't going anywhere. She had no choice but to wait until whoever had left her here returned.

Despair pressed on her.

A noise outside the cabin caught her ear. Then a squeak.

The door had opened.

She held her breath, unable to breathe.

The door opened.

Someone stepped into the room.

It was the killer Brynlee had seen on the trail when she first arrived in town.

And he was staring at her, a hungry look in his eyes.

"Which way do you want to go?" Luke asked as they stood at the trailhead that led toward the Dead Man's Bluff area.

"You and I should take the fastest way," Boone said. "The rest of the groups should pair off, and we should cover different parts of the trail."

"I agree."

Boone frowned as he considered the task before them. "I know it's a long shot. We're just guessing here. But Dead Man's Bluff is the only thing that makes sense. It's what this all goes back to."

"We should get moving then."

"That sounds like a plan." Boone glanced around at the team with him. Luke, Cruise, Abe, and Chigger. A park ranger was also there.

These were some of the best outdoorsmen Boone knew. Cruise and Abe would pair off. So would Chigger and the ranger.

"Let's go," Boone said. They didn't have any time to waste. He and Luke would take the fastest route—up the cliff near Dead Man's Bluff.

His thoughts raced as he hiked. Kat's image flashed through his mind. Then Brynlee's. Each one seemed to haunt him now.

Though he couldn't support Brynlee in the reasons she'd come here, he did care about the woman. Did that mean they could ever have a relationship? Probably not.

Yet another part of him knew he hadn't felt like this about someone in a long time.

Still, Brynlee had lied to him. How would he get past that?

"You okay back there?" Luke called over his shoulder.

"Yeah." Boone's voice sounded just above a grumble.

"I can't believe Brynlee is the one who wants to develop this mountain."

His throat burned as he heard the words spoken aloud. "Can you believe it?"

"No, not really. Did you hear her out, though?"

Boone grunted. "What's there to hear?"

"You should listen to her reasoning. You know people are complicated. She doesn't seem like the type to just do something flippantly."

"I'm not sure I'll have the chance to hear her

out." The thought caused an ache to form in his chest. He didn't want things to end like this between them.

No more tragic endings. His heart couldn't handle any more.

Luke glanced back at him. "Let's stay positive. We're going to find her."

Boone didn't say anything. Staying positive hadn't kept Kat with him. It hadn't kept his dad alive. Hadn't kept his mom at home.

"Remember when you opened your camping store?" Luke continued as they climbed up a rock formation, their path beginning a vertical trajectory.

"What about it?"

"You had about a dozen people who didn't want you to do it. They didn't want to see anything built on that stretch of road because it was their quiet fishing spot."

Boone grunted again. Yeah, he remembered that clearly. "That was different."

"Not really. You just have an emotional attachment to Dead Man's Bluff."

He wanted to deny his brother's words, but he couldn't. Dead Man's Bluff had been special because it was his and Kat's area. When she'd died . . . it had almost become like a memorial to her. To change it . . . well, it would alter his memories of his time with Kat.

He couldn't lose that part of their relationship too . . . could he?

"Don't throw away something that could be good just because of that emotional attachment," Luke continued.

They paused by the cliff leading to Dead Man's Bluff. Was his brother right? Was this fight stupid?

"Brynlee lied to me," Boone finally said. No one could deny that. And lying was a terrible way to start a relationship. Could a bond really be forged on untruths?

"You would have never gotten to know her if you'd known the truth," Luke reminded him.

Boone let out a deep breath, tired of talking about this. "We need to get moving. There's no time to waste."

"I'm going to set up on the other side of the summit. I think we'll make the best use of our time that way," Luke said.

"Be careful."

"You too."

Boone began setting up his lines so he could scale this cliff. He hoped he found Brynlee soon.

Most of all, he hoped he found her alive.

45

"You don't have to do this," Brynlee said between clenched teeth.

The man behind her didn't care. He shoved her, pushing her up the trail.

She knew exactly where they were going. Dead Man's Bluff.

It was the only place that made sense. But she also knew it was the place he planned to kill her. What she wasn't sure of was why.

"What did I ever do to you?" Brynlee asked. "Help me to understand."

She still hadn't seen the man's face. He'd come back to the cabin in costume. She couldn't make out any of his features.

That fact continued to unnerve her.

"You want to desecrate my mountain," he growled.

"I don't, though."

"You want to develop it."

"I was exploring that idea and trying to fulfill my father's wishes. But I don't want to do things the way you think. I have a better way." Was she trying to reason with someone who was unreasonable?

"I doubt that. You should have never come here." He shoved her again.

"What are you going to do with me?"

"I'm going to sacrifice you to this mountain."

"The way you sacrificed those men?"

"They also tried to desecrate this mountain."

"You've killed others throughout the years, haven't you?"

"Only the ones who disrespect the area."

"That's not your job."

"I've made it my job. No one else has volunteered."

They reached the Razor Back. The moisture left Brynlee's throat. How would she cross this without using her hands? They were still tied behind her back.

She had no other choice. The man shoved her. "Keep moving."

"How long have you been protecting this area?" she asked, taking a shaky step.

"Decades. My father did it before me."

"What about that cabin? You always keep your stuff there?"

"No one ever finds that cabin. It was the perfect place. Better than the old tree stump where I used to keep my things."

"Your plan is brilliant. Making it look like a wild animal." Brynlee's foot slipped but she righted herself. She could do this. She remembered Boone's words to her.

Boone . . . would she die never being able to ask his forgiveness?

The thought caused her heart to ache.

He'd quickly gained a place in her heart. He'd made her feel more important than anyone she'd ever dated before. The feeling of being treasured wasn't to be underestimated.

Knowing how much she'd disappointed him broke her heart.

"Keep going." The man shoved her again, nearly causing her to slide down the Razor Back. Her pulse pounded out of control.

She needed a plan. She needed something to give her hope. She couldn't just let this man take her to the top and kill her. Maybe it would be better to take her chances to slip down this mountainside.

Maybe her odds were better doing that than they were facing a certain death up top.

It was almost like the man could read her mind. He grabbed her arm with a vise-like grip. He didn't let go until they reached the top.

Brynlee glanced around.

Maybe she'd been hoping for the cavalry.

There was no one.

Just a wonderful view . . . a view that would be her death. She turned toward her captor. He'd dressed in his bear skin. Covered his face in black paint. He reached into his pocket and pulled out his claws.

And then he hissed. It was like an animal had taken over his very being.

And she knew she didn't have much time left.

Boone neared the top of the cliff. He couldn't take the chance that anyone nearby would hear him coming. No, he needed to take whoever was up there by surprise—if there was anyone up there.

If Brynlee wasn't there, Boone didn't know where he'd look for her next.

As he pulled himself onto the rock at the top, he froze.

Brynlee was there. A man stood behind her. No, a bear.

No, definitely a man dressed as a bear.

He held his claws at her throat. A look of pure terror stretched across her face.

"You don't have to do this," Boone said.

"Yes, I do."

Did he recognize that voice? He wasn't sure. It sounded vaguely familiar. The man was covered in bear skin. His face was covered in black paint.

"Why?" Boone asked.

"It's my duty."

"Let the law work these things out. Don't be a vigilante."

"The law has always failed my people."

So, he was a Native American or had Native American heritage. Many people in the area fit the bill. Who could it be?

"You killed my wife," Boone said, staring at the man.

"She wasn't supposed to see me."

"That's why you killed her? Because she saw you?"

"She came up when I was getting ready for my ceremony to Mother Earth. She saw my face."

Boone's heart lodged in his throat. "She was innocent."

"Everyone thinks they're innocent. But you should have seen the way she looked at me. It was with disgust."

"You should have given her a chance." Regret

pressed on his chest. It had been such a senseless act. Kat should be here still. "Don't make the same mistake with Brynlee. She's innocent. She's done nothing."

"She wants to destroy this place."

"She filed a permit. That doesn't mean she'll destroy anything."

"Her family . . . they kicked my family off this land."

Kicked his family off this land? Who did Boone know with family roots that went that far back?

"No more talking," the man said. "I need to end this."

"Don't do this," Brynlee said, a flash of courage in her gaze.

Boone froze, unsure where she was planning to go with this. He only hoped her words didn't provoke him. Because one wrong move would mean certain death.

"The Skookum didn't kill your father, did it?" Brynlee's voice trembled. "You've never even seen this creature."

The Skookum? Why was she bringing the Skookum up?

"Yes, it did!" The man snapped. "The Skookum are real."

"Your family was the Skookum, weren't they?" Brynlee continued. "When your relatives saw my family on the land that they thought belonged to them, they began to tell stories about how evil these newcomers were. They needed a way to protect this land, so your dad started pretending to be a Skookum. Maybe other people in your family did the same."

Brynlee wasn't making sense . . . or was she?

Boone sucked in a quick breath. He realized who was behind this.

There was only one person in town obsessed with the Skookum. Who had wanted to keep that legend alive.

Fowler.

46

How could Fowler be behind this? Brynlee wondered. The man had crept in under the radar. He'd been unassuming.

Yet he'd been in front of them the whole time. He'd heard their plans. He'd fed the stories about the Skookum. He knew this land.

Now he was going to kill her.

Boone was going to have to watch it.

He'd probably die too.

And there was nothing anyone could do to stop it.

Brynlee swallowed a scream of despair.

"Now you're going to pay!" Fowler said behind her.

He raised his claws.

Brynlee braced herself for the pain she was sure

would come. She waited to feel the sharp claws pierce her skin. For breath to leave her lungs.

"I'm sorry, Boone," she muttered.

His face tightened, and his eyes became orbs of sorrow.

He was sorry too, wasn't he? Maybe there was even a chance he'd forgive her.

But would it be too late?

She closed her eyes and braced herself.

Instead of pain, she heard something behind her.

A pop. A grunt. A sudden intake of air.

She froze.

Waited.

Anticipated.

What had just happened?

Fowler's grip on her loosened. Brynlee took a step away. She glanced back and saw the man sink to the ground, his body limp.

What? It didn't matter. All that mattered was that he was no longer holding her captive.

At the realization, Brynlee's muscles turned to jelly. Her sudden relief made her feel lightheaded.

Before she hit the ground, Boone's arms scooped beneath her. Lifted her up. Picked her up and carried her away from the scene with Fowler.

Brynlee looked back in time to see his body on the ground. Luke stood behind them, a gun in his hand. He must have come up the other side of the cliff.

His men arrived and rushed toward Fowler to secure the scene.

She was okay. She was really okay.

Tears streamed down her face, and she buried her head in Boone's shoulder.

"I've got you," he whispered.

And Brynlee knew he did.

This was over. It was really over.

Three hours later, law enforcement was still scouring Dead Man's Bluff. Luke had cleared Boone to walk Brynlee back down.

Thank goodness. Because all she wanted was a shower. A warm place to rest. Some tea.

And maybe a conversation with Boone.

They were quiet as they started down the trail. As soon as they were out of sight from everyone else, Boone paused. He took her into his arms and held her tight.

"I thought I was going to lose you," he murmured.

Brynlee burrowed herself in his embrace, relishing the feel of his strong arms around her. "I'm sorry, Boone. I never meant for things to happen like this. I didn't know until I came here just how special this area was. I was only trying to follow my father's last wishes. I thought if I could do this that maybe I'd find a place with my half-brothers. Maybe I'd have the family I'd always craved."

"You should have told me."

Brynlee stepped back and stared into his green eyes—eyes that she'd quickly fallen in love with. "Then you would have never spoken to me. We would have never gotten to know each other. You can't argue with that fact."

Boone scowled but didn't deny her words.

She decided to continue. He hadn't run yet. Maybe he would listen now. "I have some conceptual drawings back in my SUV that show the original dream my father created. I've been afraid you would find them and my secret would be revealed. His plans were for a full-fledged resort with thirty rooms and a restaurant. But I have a different idea."

Boone's jaw tightened, as if he was reining in his emotions. "What's that?"

"It's something that I think can be a win-win for everyone." Brynlee drew in a deep breath before blurting, "I'd like to open a sky lift to the top."

He blanched, as if her words had surprised him. "What?"

She nodded, excitement building in her. "A sky lift wouldn't be that intrusive on the mountain. But it *would* allow people who've never seen a view like this to see it. Plus, it would help preserve the beauty of the area."

"Hmm . . ." Boone remained silent a moment, as if processing the idea. "I don't know what to say."

She rested a hand on his chest, desperate to get through to him. "There's more. I'd like to purchase some of the land near your store for parking."

"What?" His eyes narrowed as he waited for her to continue.

"It's too early to say for sure, but I think the best area for going up the mountain will be not far from your store. But we'd need parking. You've got the space."

"But . . ."

"And this would help you." Excitement built in her voice. "The money we'd pay you could help secure the mountain. In fact, we'd probably need to secure that mountain before we could proceed. It could become our problem instead of yours."

"Really? I don't know what to say."

"I mean, I know it's all still early. But I think it could work. If the town approves it."

He tugged her closer. "I like that idea."

"You do?" Surprise echoed in Brynlee's voice as tears rushed to her eyes. She'd hoped and prayed she might get through to him with this idea, and right now Boone wasn't running away. He wasn't critiquing it. He looked like he might actually like it.

Joy burst inside her.

"I do. And I think Kat would approve also. She loved that view. She'd want other people to see it also." Boone lowered his voice. "I'm sorry I didn't let you explain."

"I'm sorry I didn't tell you."

He drew in a deep breath, still staring deeply into her eyes. "Brynlee, you've . . . you've ignited something in me that I haven't felt in a long time. I know you have a life back in Pennsylvania but . . . I'm not ready to walk away from us."

"From us?" Her voice lilted with surprise this time. "There's an us?"

"I mean, I know that sounds presumptuous." He raised a shoulder, not in uncertainty but in playful hope.

"No, I like it." Brynlee grinned. "I like the sound of that."

"You do?"

"I do."

He pulled her closer. "I'm glad to hear that. And I want you to know you have a community here, Brynlee. You don't need to try so hard to find approval with your half-brothers."

"I think the town hates me."

"Give them time. I know they'll see the best in you also. My family has your back."

Tears streamed down her face at his words. "That sounds amazing."

Boone pushed a hair out of her face, his gaze studying her as deep affection filled his eyes. "I think . . . I think we should see where this goes, Brynlee. I never thought I'd say those words again after Kat died. I never thought I would want this again. Like I said, I know you have a life back in Pennsylvania—"

"I may be spending a lot more time here, depending on how things go," Brynlee said. His words seemed to crack something open inside her. Longing and warmth spread through her.

Boone smiled. "I like the sound of that."

As the forest surrounded them, it suddenly didn't feel as scary. No, it seemed more like a fortress, something that the world needed to see. Boone lowered his lips until they met hers . . . and everything else disappeared.

EPILOGUE

Boone put his arm around Brynlee as he watched the crews start to work. A group of thirty or so people had gathered for the ribbon cutting ceremony here at the base of the mountain. Mostly it was town officials and those who had a stake in making this happen.

After several rounds of negotiations, the county had approved the sky lift to the top of Dead Man's Bluff. It would have minimal invasiveness to the land, bring in more visitors to Fog Lake, and showcase this area's beauty.

The road to get here hadn't been easy. There had still been pushback to get the permits needed. It had required surveys and engineering plans. A few locals still didn't want the mountain to be touched and had protested.

But everything had worked out.

Best of all, Brynlee was staying in Fog Lake to oversee everything. She and Boone had practically been inseparable over the past several months. Their time together had been more than he could hope for—a treasure and an answer to prayer.

"Here it is," Boone murmured into her ear. "Your father's dream."

A soft smile feathered across Brynlee's lips as she stared at the side of the mountain in front of them. "I just wish he was here to see it."

A small crowd had gathered to watch the opening day of construction. They stood in the new parking lot near Boone's store. The county had approved the space, Brynlee's father's company had purchased the land, and building the lot had been one of the first orders of business.

Securing the mountain to make it safe for everyone around had also been a priority.

"It took a lot to get here, didn't it?" Brynlee squeezed him tighter as she draped her arm around his waist. "I wasn't sure this would ever happen."

"I know what you're talking about."

The past several months had been a whirlwind. Not only with trying to get this approved but with wrapping up the case against Fowler.

The police had discovered that Fowler's father had been acting as a Skookum since Fowler was a child. Fowler had picked up the torch after his father had passed away. His Native American roots to this area had made him feel overly protective of this land. A psychologist had also said he wrestled with mental illness, though he concealed it well.

He had more than one bear costume that he'd created himself. He also had special shoes that made his tracks look like bear prints.

Big Ben had been a scapegoat. Fowler knew about the man's love of bears. He sent a note, asking Big Ben to be outside Brynlee's chalet the night that Fowler had thrown the axes. Fowler had paid Big Ben two hundred dollars, knowing he was the perfect person to set up to take the fall since the man didn't speak and was chronically stoic.

Fowler had also been the one who'd gone into Falling Timbers that day and who'd knocked Chigger out. He'd apparently been planning on killing Brynlee right then. But his conscience had kicked in, and he'd changed his mind.

Fowler's hatred toward Brynlee's father's family went back a long way.

His family had claimed that the Brinkleys stole their land when they purchased it eighty years ago. When he discovered that the person who'd seen him kill those two hikers on the trail was not only planning to develop the mountain but that she was a Brinkley . . . he'd come unhinged.

Boone looked over as more people joined them at the site. Aside from town officials, Luke and Harper were here, along with Ansley, Chigger, and Abe. It was great to have a support system here to stand beside them.

Even county inspector Todd Michaels had shown up. He hadn't exactly congratulated them, but Boone knew this was a victory. Todd could no longer threaten to shut down his store. He'd have to wait for other ways to try to make Boone miserable.

"Excuse me," someone said behind them.

Boone turned. His eyes widened when he saw Kat's mom there.

"Nancy . . ." Boone started. He took a step toward her, wondering if she'd come to cause trouble. The last thing he wanted was to ruin Brynlee's big day.

The woman frowned and dabbed the corner of her eye with a tissue. "I just wanted to say I'm sorry for blaming you. My daughter loved you very much. We focused our grief on the wrong thing in an effort to make ourselves feel better. Katherine wouldn't have wanted that."

Shock washed through him. Boone had never in a million years thought this day would come. Instantly, some kind of healing seemed to flush through him. "I appreciate that."

Nancy nodded at both of them, more tears

escaping down her cheeks. "Best of luck with this project. And, again . . . I'm sorry."

"Nancy . . ." Boone called.

She paused and turned. Boone pulled her into a hug, and the woman melted with sobs. Boone couldn't keep the tears from his own eyes. Maybe this was the beginning of a restoration that was a long time coming.

He waited until Nancy pulled away. She patted his arms, nodded, and walked back to join the crowds in the distance.

As Boone returned to Brynlee, she smiled up at him. The look of love and support in her eyes filled him to the brim with completeness. It had been a long, hard journey to get here, but he was so grateful to have arrived.

"That was unexpected, huh?" she said quietly.

"You can say that again." His voice caught as he remembered Nancy's words. He'd craved for reconciliation with Katherine's family for so long.

"I'm glad you have some closure, Boone."

He tightened his arm around her waist. "Me too. I'm glad you got some closure with your half-brothers."

Mason Brinkley himself had come into town and given his stamp of approval on the project. Boone hadn't exactly liked the man . . . but at least their exchanges had been pleasant.

Mason had told them he'd come into town to follow up on what Brynlee was doing, that he didn't trust his half-sister to oversee the project. He was upset because he'd wanted to take charge of the project himself and he had, in fact, come into town several times over the past several years, hoping to scope out the area for a possible resort.

"Me too," Brynlee said. "I'll never really be a part of their family. I don't fit. But I'm okay with that. I've found a new community here, a community that's not my own flesh and blood. Sometimes your support system doesn't have to be your blood relatives."

Boone kissed her forehead. "No, it doesn't. Besides, Luke and Harper are ready to adopt you into the family."

Brynlee smiled. "I like that."

"So do I."

"There's one other thing I wanted to tell you." Brynlee stepped backed and looked up into his eyes. "We're going to preserve your tree. We've named it Katherine's Tree, and it will be one of the features at the top of Dead Man's Bluff. It will be a great way to remember her and to remember how much she loved this area."

Tears rushed to Boone's eyes as her words washed over him. "Really?"

"Really."

He pulled Brynlee toward him and wrapped his arms around her. "Thank you, Brynlee."

"I wanted to do something so the past wasn't forgotten. I know that's important to you."

"You're important to me." He stepped back and cupped her face with his hand. "I love you, Brynlee Parker."

A grin spread across her face. "I love you too."

Their lips met. Boone knew that what he wanted more than anything for the rest of his life was to share more moments like these. And there was no better place to do so than this breathtaking area they both now called home.

ALSO BY CHRISTY BARRITT:

IF YOU ENJOYED THIS BOOK, YOU ALSO MIGHT ENJOY:

LANTERN BEACH MYSTERIES

Hidden Currents

You can take the detective out of the investigation, but you can't take the investigator out of the detective. A notorious gang puts a bounty on Detective Cady Matthews's head after she takes down their leader, leaving her no choice but to hide until she can testify at trial. But her temporary home across the country on a remote North Carolina island isn't as peaceful as she initially thinks. Living under the new identity of Cassidy Livingston, she struggles to keep her investigative skills tucked away, especially after a body washes ashore. When local police bungle the murder investigation, she can't resist stepping in. But Cassidy is supposed to be keeping a low profile. One wrong move could lead to both her discovery and her demise. Can she bring justice to the island . . . or will the hidden currents surrounding her pull her under for good?

Flood Watch

The tide is high, and so is the danger on Lantern Beach. Still in hiding after infiltrating a dangerous gang, Cassidy Livingston just has to make it a few more months before she can testify at trial and resume her old life. But trouble keeps finding her, and Cassidy is pulled into a local investigation after a man mysteriously disappears from the island she now calls home. A recurring nightmare from her time undercover only muddies things, as does a visit from the parents of her handsome ex-Navy SEAL neighbor. When a friend's life is threatened, Cassidy must make choices that put her on the verge of blowing her cover. With a flood watch on her emotions and her life in a tangle, will Cassidy find the truth? Or will her past finally drown her?

Storm Surge

A storm is brewing hundreds of miles away, but its effects are devastating even from afar. Laid-back, loose, and light: that's Cassidy Livingston's new motto. But when a makeshift boat with a bloody cloth inside washes ashore near her oceanfront home, her detective instincts shift into gear . . . again. Seeking clues isn't the only thing on her mind—romance is heating up with next-door neighbor and former Navy SEAL Ty Chambers as well. Her heart wants the love and stability she's longed for her entire life. But her hidden identity only leads to a tidal wave of turbulence. As more answers emerge about the boat, the danger around her rises, creating a treacherous swell that threatens to reveal her past. Can Cassidy mind her own business, or will the storm surge of violence and corruption that has washed ashore on Lantern Beach leave her life in wreckage?

Dangerous Waters

Danger lurks on the horizon, leaving only two choices: find shelter or flee. Cassidy Livingston's new identity has begun to feel as comfortable as her favorite sweater. She's been tucked away on Lantern Beach for weeks, waiting to testify against a deadly gang, and is settling in to a new life she wants to last forever. When she thinks she spots someone malevolent from her past, panic swells inside her. If an enemy has found her, Cassidy won't be the only one who's a target. Everyone she's come to love will also be at risk. Dangerous waters threaten to pull her into an overpowering chasm she may never escape. Can Cassidy survive what lies ahead? Or has the tide fatally turned against her?

Perilous Riptide

Just when the current seems safer, an unseen danger emerges and threatens to destroy everything. When Cassidy Livingston finds a journal hidden deep in the recesses of her ice cream truck, her curiosity kicks into high gear. Islanders suspect that Elsa, the journal's owner, didn't die accidentally. Her final entry indicates their suspicions might be correct and that what Elsa observed on her final night may have led to her demise. Against the advice of Ty Chambers, her former Navy SEAL boyfriend, Cassidy taps into her detective skills and hunts for answers. But her search only leads to a skeletal body and trouble for both of them. As helplessness threatens to drown her, Cassidy is desperate to turn back time. Can Cassidy find what she needs to navigate the perilous situation? Or will the riptide surrounding her threaten everyone and everything Cassidy loves?

Deadly Undertow

The current's fatal pull is powerful, but so is one detective's will to live. When someone from Cassidy Livingston's past shows up on Lantern Beach and warns her of impending peril, opposing currents collide, threatening to drag her under. Running would be easy. But leaving would break her heart. Cassidy must decipher between the truth and lies, between reality and deception. Even more importantly, she must decide whom to trust and whom to fear. Her life depends on it. As danger rises and answers surface, everything Cassidy thought she knew is tested. In order to survive, Cassidy must take drastic measures and end the battle against the ruthless gang DH-7 once and for all. But if her final mission fails, the consequences will be as deadly as the raging undertow.

LANTERN BEACH ROMANTIC SUSPENSE

Tides of Deception

Change has come to Lantern Beach: a new police chief, a new season, and . . . a new romance? Austin Brooks has loved Skye Lavinia from the moment they met, but the walls she keeps around her seem impenetrable. Skye knows Austin is the best thing to ever happen to her. Yet she also knows that if he learns the truth about her past, he'd be a fool not to run. A chance encounter brings secrets bubbling to the surface, and danger soon follows. Are the life-threatening events plaguing them really accidents . . . or is someone trying to send a deadly message? With the tides on Lantern Beach come deception and lies. One question remains—who will be swept away as the water shifts? And will it bring the end for Austin and Skye, or merely the beginning?

Shadow of Intrigue

For her entire life, Lisa Garth has felt like a supporting character in the drama of life. The designation never bothered her—until now. Lantern Beach, where she's settled and runs a popular restaurant, has boarded up for the season. The slower pace leaves her with too much time alone. Braden Dillinger came to Lantern Beach to try to heal. The former Special Forces officer returned from battle with invisible scars and diminished hope. But his recovery is hampered by the fact that an unknown enemy is trying to kill him. From the moment Lisa and Braden meet, danger ignites around them, and both are drawn into a web of intrigue that turns their lives upside down. As shadows creep in, will Lisa and Braden be able to shine a light on the peril around them? Or will the encroaching darkness turn their worst nightmares into reality?

Storm of Doubt

A pastor who's lost faith in God. A romance writer who's lost faith in love. A faceless man with a deadly obsession. Nothing has felt right in Pastor Jack Wilson's world since his wife died two years ago. He hoped coming to Lantern Beach might help soothe the ragged edges of his soul. Instead, he feels more alone than ever. Novelist Juliette Grace came to the island to hide away. Though her professional life has never been better, her personal life has imploded. Her husband left her and a stalker's threats have grown more and more dangerous. When Jack saves Juliette from an attack, he sees the terror in her gaze and knows he must protect her. But when danger strikes again, will Jack be able to keep her safe? Or will the approaching storm prove too strong to withstand?

LANTERN BEACH PD

On the Lookout

When Cassidy Chambers accepted the job as police chief on Lantern Beach, she knew the island had its secrets. But a suspicious death with potentially far-reaching implications will test all her skills —and threaten to reveal her true identity. Cassidy enlists the help of her husband, former Navy SEAL Ty Chambers. As they dig for answers, both uncover parts of their pasts that are best left buried. Not everything is as it seems, and they must figure out if their John Doe is connected to the secretive group that has moved onto the island. As facts materialize, danger on the island grows. Can Cassidy and Ty discover the truth about the shadowy crimes in their cozy community? Or has darkness permanently invaded their beloved Lantern Beach?

Attempt to Locate

A fun girls' night out turns into a nightmare when armed robbers barge into the store where Cassidy and her friends are shopping. As the situation escalates and the men escape, a massive manhunt launches on Lantern Beach to apprehend the dangerous trio. In the midst of the chaos, a potential foe asks for Cassidy's help. He needs to find his sister who fled from the secretive Gilead's Cove community on the island. But the more Cassidy learns about the seemingly untouchable group, the more her unease grows. The pressure to solve both cases continues to mount. But as the gravity of the situation rises, so does the danger. Cassidy is determined to protect the island and break up the cult . . . but doing so might cost her everything.

First Degree Murder

Police Chief Cassidy Chambers longs for a break from the recent crimes plaguing Lantern Beach. She simply wants to enjoy her friends' upcoming wedding, to prepare for the busy tourist season about to slam the island, and to gather all the dirt she can on the suspicious community that's invaded the town. But trouble explodes on the island, sending residents—including Cassidy—into a squall of uneasiness. Cassidy may have more than one enemy plotting her demise, and the collateral damage seems unthinkable. As the temperature rises, so does the pressure to find answers. Someone is determined that Lantern Beach would be better off without their new police chief. And for Cassidy, one wrong move could mean certain death.

Dead on Arrival

With a highly charged local election consuming the community, Police Chief Cassidy Chambers braces herself for a challenging day of breaking up petty conflicts and tamping down high emotions. But when widespread food poisoning spreads among potential voters across the island, Cassidy smells something rotten in the air. As Cassidy examines every possibility to uncover what's going on, local enigma Anthony Gilead again comes on her radar. The man is running for mayor and his cult-like following is growing at an alarming rate. Cassidy feels certain he has a spy embedded in her inner circle. The problem is that her pool of suspects gets deeper every day. Can Cassidy get to the bottom of what's eating away at her peaceful island home? Will voters turn out despite the outbreak of illness plaguing their tranquil town? And the even bigger question: Has darkness come to stay on Lantern Beach?

THE SQUEAKY CLEAN MYSTERIES:

On her way to completing a degree in forensic science, Gabby St. Claire drops out of school and starts her own crime-scene cleaning business. When a routine cleaning job uncovers a murder weapon the police overlooked, she realizes that the wrong person is in jail. She also realizes that crime scene cleaning might be the perfect career for utilizing her investigative skills.

HOLLY ANNA PALADIN MYSTERIES:

When Holly Anna Paladin is given a year to live, she embraces her final days doing what she loves most—random acts of kindness. But when one of her extreme good deeds goes horribly wrong, implicating Holly in a string of murders, Holly is suddenly in a different kind of fight for her life. She knows one thing for sure: she only has a short amount of time to make a difference. And if helping the people she cares about puts her in danger, it's a risk worth taking.

THE WORST DETECTIVE EVER:

I'm not really a private detective. I just play one on TV.

Joey Darling, better known to the world as Raven Remington, detective extraordinaire, is trying to separate herself from her invincible alter ego. She played the spunky character for five years on the hit TV show *Relentless*, which catapulted her to fame and into the role of Hollywood's sweetheart. When her marriage falls apart, her finances dwindle to nothing, and her father disappears, Joey finds herself on the Outer Banks of North Carolina, trying to piece together her life away from the limelight. But as people continually mistake her for the character she played on TV, she's tasked with solving real life crimes . . . even though she's terrible at it.

ABOUT THE AUTHOR

USA Today has called Christy Barritt's books "scary, funny, passionate, and quirky."

Christy writes both mystery and romantic suspense novels that are clean with underlying messages of faith. Her books have won the Daphne du Maurier Award for Excellence in Suspense and Mystery, have been twice nominated for the Romantic Times Reviewers' Choice Award, and have finaled for both a Carol Award and Foreword Magazine's Book of the Year.

She is married to her Prince Charming, a man who thinks she's hilarious—but only when she's not trying to be. Christy is a self-proclaimed klutz, an avid music lover who's known for spontaneously bursting into song, and a road trip aficionado.

When she's not working or spending time with her family, she enjoys singing, playing the guitar, and exploring small, unsuspecting towns where people have no idea how accident-prone she is.

Find Christy online at:
www.christybarritt.com
www.facebook.com/christybarritt
www.twitter.com/cbarritt

Sign up for Christy's newsletter to get information on all of her latest releases here: **www. christybarritt.com/newsletter-sign-up/**

If you enjoyed this book, please consider leaving a review.

Made in the USA
San Bernardino, CA
21 July 2019